Lionhearts

THE PRIDE OF AMSTERDAM

ELIZABETH COLDWELL

The Pride of Amsterdam
ISBN # 978-1-78430-383-9
©Copyright Elizabeth Coldwell 2014
Cover Art by Posh Gosh ©Copyright December 2014
Interior text design by Claire Siemaszkiewicz
Totally Bound Publishing

THE PRIDE OF AMSTERDAM

Dedication

To everyone who makes spending time in Amsterdam
such a pleasure.

Prologue

December 31st, 1999

It was a fine night for the end of the world.

Kees shivered in his thin jacket and wondered again why he'd let Johnny talk him into coming to this party. He didn't do parties, hated being stranded in a room full of strangers while his lively, charming best friend navigated effortlessly toward the most gorgeous girls in the room. But tonight was different, as Johnny kept telling him. Millennium Eve — the night when — if the news media was correct — some bug would cause computer systems to fail across the globe. Cash machines would stop giving out money, planes would fall from the sky, and nuclear missiles would be launched from army bases.

"And when all of that happens, you can't worry about it, Kees. You can just drink and dance, right?" he had said, that infectious grin of his spreading across his face.

Johnny had heard about the party from someone who'd come into the record shop on Kalverstraat where he worked. It was being held in one of the big, abandoned warehouses out in the Eastern Docklands, where squatters lived. In the last few years, many of the buildings here had been knocked down or redeveloped, as this part of the city was transformed by degrees into a modern vista of apartments and office blocks, and most of those squatting in them had been driven away. But a few die-hards remained, refusing to leave until they were forced out, their residences daubed with political slogans and colorful graffiti. The squatters claimed this development wasn't about what was best for the ordinary people of Amsterdam, but for the property speculators. Johnny didn't necessarily sympathize with their ideology. He just believed their parties were the place to meet the best girls and score the best dope.

"Is it much farther now?" Kees looked around him as they trudged down the road that ran alongside the dock. Points of light, reflections from the few occupied buildings around them, glimmered in the dark water. There were plans to extend one of the tram services out here, to cater for the residents of these new homes, but that work would not be complete till years from now, and tonight they'd had to walk most of the way.

"Just up ahead, I promise." Johnny, who'd been walking a little distance ahead of Kees, clearly eager to reach their destination, turned back and regarded him, blond head cocked to one side. "Come on, Kees. Lighten up. This is going to be fun. I mean, what was your other option tonight? Sitting at home with your mother and your *oma* Annie, watching some lame variety show on TV?"

Kees shrugged. Since his grandmother had moved in with them, that pretty much described every Saturday night in the van der Veer household. Johnny was right. He needed to get out more, have fun. Maybe meet someone special. The last thought caused his heart to sink again. How was he ever going to have a relationship with anyone if he couldn't be honest about what he wanted? He'd known for a long time now that he was gay, but he hadn't been able to share that knowledge with anyone—not his mother, not Johnny, not even any of the school counselors who'd been on hand throughout his education, ready to deal with whatever problems the students might encounter. At eighteen, he was sure he was the only one in his circle of friends who'd never been on a date and the longer he waited, the more difficult it became to admit what he really wanted.

"Yeah, that would have been pretty grim." Up ahead, he heard the sound of music and voices raised in raucous laughter. "Hey, that must be the place, right?"

"Right. Let's go..." Johnny broke into a trot, obviously eager to be inside now they'd reached their destination.

Kees followed him, telling himself with a confidence that he did not feel that this would be okay. By the time he'd caught up with Johnny, his friend was in a big, backslapping embrace with a denim-clad guy who had piercings in his left ear and upper lip.

"Glad you could make it, man," Pierced Guy drawled. He had a strong American accent, though Kees couldn't have said what part of the States he was from. Turning his attention to Kees, he said, "And this is the friend you were telling me about, right?"

"Yeah, this is Kees. Kees, this is Tyler. He was just telling me his band's playing the Paradiso next month, and he can get us on the guest list. How cool is that?"

Kees wanted to point out that if everything Johnny had said about this computer super-bug were true, there wasn't going to be a next month, but he just nodded. "Yeah, that sounds like fun."

"We'll catch you later," Johnny told Tyler. "Let's go get a drink, Kees."

They made their way into the warehouse's dimly lit interior. Nirvana's *Smells Like Teen Spirit* blasted from stereo speakers at a volume that made conversation all but impossible. Kees wrinkled his nose at the overpowering stink of dope smoke and spicy cooking smells. The squatters had managed to keep the electricity and plumbing connected, but the big windows were covered in grime, the floorboards creaked beneath his feet and the building gave off a general air of neglect. He might not enjoy living with his mother and elderly grandmother, but this anarchic lifestyle held just as little appeal for him.

Off the main hall, they found the room that acted as a makeshift kitchen. On a rickety table stood an assortment of bottles and cans, and a big metal bowl containing a dubious-looking liquid in which slices of orange and apple floated. They added their own contribution—a bottle of cheap vodka that they had bought from a night shop on the way out to the Docklands—to what Johnny called with a laugh "the drinks cabinet". Then he grabbed two paper cups and dipped them into the punchbowl to fill them, before handing one to Kees.

One sip told Kees the punch was mostly alcohol, with a little fruit juice for flavor. It wouldn't take much of this to get him drunk, but Johnny was knocking back his own cup with enthusiasm.

"Let me fill these up again," Johnny said, "and then we'll go and mingle."

Kees could have happily stayed here in the kitchen all night, away from the pounding music and the people with whom he'd have nothing in common. But he watched as Johnny scooped up more punch, then trailed after his friend, back out into heart of the party.

In the center of the room, a group of young men were dancing to the music, pushing and jostling each other and singing in full-throated fashion to Kurt Cobain's words of alienation and despair. Kees and Johnny took up a position against one wall, not wanting to get sucked into the whirling vortex of dancers.

A girl wandered over, tall and blonde, in a paisley patterned dress that revealed most of her long, bare legs. She held a tightly rolled joint in one hand. "Do you have a light?" she asked Johnny.

He made a show of patting his jeans pockets, looking for his lighter. He'd once told Kees it was a move designed to draw a woman's attention to your bulge. Kees had never believed it would work, until he saw the way the blonde's gaze appeared fixed on the tight, faded denim that covered his friend's crotch. At last, Johnny retrieved his Zippo and flicked the case open in one smooth movement.

The girl bent close, the roll-up held between her lips, and waited for the tip to catch alight. Standing up, she took a long inhale, the corners of her mouth quirking up in satisfaction.

"You want a hit?" She held the joint out to Johnny.

He dragged on it, coughing a little as he drew down the smoke, but nodding to show her the sensation was pleasurable. He made to pass it on to Kees.

"No, thanks. I'm good," Kees assured him.

The blonde regarded Johnny from beneath lowered eyelids. "I need some fresh air. Why don't we go outside, see if we can see any fireworks?"

Kees knew he wasn't included in the invitation. When Johnny looked at him, he said, "You go. Have fun. I'm fine here, honestly."

"You sure?" Johnny seemed torn between concern at abandoning Kees and eagerness to let the blonde lead him out into the night.

"Yeah." He grinned. "If you're not back by midnight, I'll come find you, so we can look at the planes falling out of the sky like you promised."

Johnny and the girl walked away. They didn't even reach the doorway before they had their arms round each other and were sharing a deep, spit-swapping kiss. Kees tried to suppress a pang of envy. Johnny had no inhibitions, nothing to stop him getting what he wanted. Why couldn't Kees be so carefree, so unafraid of what the consequences might be if he admitted that he really wanted the same kind of easy connection with a lover?

"You look like you'd rather be anywhere than here."

The voice at his ear surprised him. He turned to see a man who must have been a good six and a half feet in height — tall even by Dutch standards — with a mane of corn-blond hair that he pushed away from his face with one hand. The stranger's eyes, of a shade Kees had never seen before — somewhere between amber and gold — regarded him with something very like sympathy.

"I'm just not a great one for parties, that's all," Kees mumbled. Always shy around people he didn't know, he found his throat drying and the hairs on his neck prickling in response to the man's presence. More than that, he was all too conscious of a sudden tension in his groin. He felt his cock thicken and grow. He blushed, unable to prevent his body's response to being in the presence of someone so masculine, so vital, so...arousing.

"And yet here you are," the stranger commented.

"Well, I came because my friend wanted to, but he's just hooked up with a girl. And I'm really not very good at making conversation with people I don't know very well."

"There are other things one can do than make conversation." Again, his new companion ran a hand through his glorious mass of hair and fixed Kees with a stare that held him rooted to the spot. He'd never had such an instant, powerful reaction to anyone, and all he wanted to do was to sink to his knees and obey this man's every wish.

"I don't— That is, I..." he stammered.

The man put a finger to Kees' lips, gently silencing him. Kees fought the urge to take that digit between his lips and suck.

"What is your name?"

"Kees."

"Did you know you're really cute when you blush, Kees?"

The observation sent the flush back to his cheeks, harder than before. He shivered, aware of the man's strong physical presence and seductive, musky smell. That scent didn't come out of a bottle. He knew it to be pure, primal male, and he wanted to breathe it in forever.

"This is a big building," his companion said casually. "I'm sure we can find somewhere a little quieter. Somewhere we can be alone."

Kees took a gulp of his punch, no longer flinching at the strength of the alcohol. He needed all the courage he could muster to agree to such a blatant proposition. His jeans had grown uncomfortably tight, struggling to contain the urgent swelling of his dick, and more than anything he wanted to be somewhere private, where he could bare himself to this man. Yet still he hesitated.

"Don't be afraid, Kees. I'm not going to ask of you anything you're not prepared to offer. But let me give you just a little taste of what I have in mind..."

He bent his head, and put his mouth to Kees'. When he ran his tongue along the seam of Kees' lips, there was no resisting the gentle pressure.

The room seemed to dissolve around them as they kissed. Kees could no longer hear the music that had been assaulting his eardrums or see the wild, uncoordinated dancing. He was lost in the softness of this stranger's mouth and as their bodies pressed together, he could feel the man's erection up against his belly. He wanted to reach down and grasp it through its denim covering, but that seemed like entirely too forward an act.

When they broke the kiss, his companion smiled down at him. "You taste good. And you kiss well, too."

"It was my first kiss." Kees didn't know why he felt the need to admit that.

"There's no shame in admitting to that. And it's always an honor to be someone's first..."

The implication in those words could not be ignored. Kees thought of all the other firsts that awaited him. Seeing a lover naked, caressing his body, sucking and being sucked, the thrill of penetration...

He'd always thought that each of those steps would be part of a long, slow procession to the ultimate destination. But now it didn't seem like waiting—

taking his time — made any sense. If Johnny was right, and the world did end tonight, Kees didn't want to die regretting the things he hadn't done.

"Okay, let's go," he said.

They pushed their way through the crush of bodies, out into a long corridor and up a spiral staircase with black-painted iron treads. This took them up to a balcony level, where they found a room that Kees presumed had once been an office. It acted as a bedroom now, with a bare mattress on the floor and some clothes hanging on a line strung between two exposed pipes. Not exactly the environment he'd pictured for his first time.

Kees found himself being pressed up against the wall and kissed again, with more intensity than before. He plucked at the man's shirt, frantic in his haste to undo the buttons. The garment parted to reveal an expanse of broad, lightly furred chest that he yearned to run his tongue along. Already, he could get a whiff of his companion's scent, undisguised by the artificial aromas of soap and cologne. The man smelled of musk and the forest floor, and Kees thought he could breathe him in forever.

"Got to get you out of those clothes," his lover murmured.

Kees went limp as he was relieved of his jacket and sweater, the layers that he'd worn in a vain attempt to keep warm on the walk to the squat now seeming unnecessary and cumbersome. His companion tossed the clothes to the none-too-clean floor. His jeans soon followed. Kees shrugged them down and off his skinny hips. He was all too aware that his tight, white briefs did nothing to conceal his excited state. The fabric clung to the curve of his uncoiled dick, and a damp spot had formed where his pre-cum seeped through.

"I see you're ready for me." The man—God, Kees wished he knew what to call him, but he'd made no effort to share that information and this didn't seem like the time to ask—traced a finger over the swelling erection. It stiffened further at his touch. He pulled the cotton down, letting that hard length spring free. Kees shuddered with desire and shame at being so exposed, stripped down for another man's pleasure.

"You have a gorgeous cock..."

Kees sucked in a breath as long, cool fingers grasped his shaft. No one had ever touched him there, and he felt too shy to offer any kind of instructions as to how he liked to be stroked. But somehow this man, who looked to have around five or six years in age on him and so much more experience, already knew. Maybe all men just wanted the same thing, those hard, direct back-and-forth tugs. Each one had him rising up on his toes and panting with need.

Already, he was on the edge. Any more of this treatment, and he would be squirting his cum over his companion's hand. He looked into those bizarre golden eyes, which seemed to regard him with both arousal and amusement. "Please, I don't think I can take any more."

"Then tell me what you want me to do instead."

"I—I want you to fuck me."

"Are you sure?"

He'd never been so sure of anything in his young life. "Of course."

"Then lie down on the mattress."

Kees did as he'd been told, even though the striped ticking was stained and didn't smell too good.

Someone sleeps here every night with no qualms, he reminded himself. *Don't be so squeamish.*

His lover stood in front of him, undoing his olive cord trousers. He wore no underwear, and Kees marveled at the size of the man's dick. How would he be able to accommodate something so big without being split in two?

"Don't worry. I'll take it slowly." The words reassured him a bit, as he was joined on the mattress.

The two fell into each other's arms. Kees stroked and caressed every inch of his lover's skin he could reach. He squirmed as the man licked a wet trail over each nipple in turn, before moving down to lap at the little hollow of his belly button.

"Ticklish, huh?" The words were punctuated by a deep chuckle. "I'll be sure to remember that."

Remember it? Does that mean we'll be doing this again? The feel of that supple tongue being played over the insides of his thighs caused Kees to lose his already tenuous grip on the thought and surrender to the thrill of being licked. He didn't object as he was rolled over so that he lay face down, his bare backside sticking up in the air.

His companion pushed Kees' legs apart. Each of his arse cheeks was kissed in turn, then he was being licked in the crease between them. Even in his most fevered fantasy, he'd never imagined anyone doing anything so rude to him, but it was sheer bliss. Kees clutched at the piped edging of the mattress, feeling pleasure unwind low in his belly. Without being aware he was going to do it, he thrust his rump back at his lover, desperate for the man's tongue to make contact with his arsehole.

When it did, he almost screamed. He felt the sensation in every part of his body, from his scalp to

Elizabeth Coldwell

his toes. How could such a depraved act be so good, so...right? He didn't know, and he didn't care—just as long as it kept on happening, kept on bringing him the kind of joy he'd only ever dreamed of.

All too soon, that delicious tongue was withdrawn. In its place, a fingertip, wet with saliva, was pressed to the puckered bud.

"Let's see how ready you are," his lover muttered, as he pushed his finger knuckle-deep into Kees' arse. "Oh, yes, you're almost there. Let's just see if you can take another finger..."

He kept up a running commentary as he inserted a second digit alongside the first, telling Kees how hot and tight his arse was, and how good it felt to be fucking him this way. Kees grunted in response, strangely pleased with himself for being able to take two fingers without complaint.

Some of his reservations came back when the fingers were pulled out. Kees looked over his shoulder to see the man reach out a hand to grab his discarded trousers. He pulled out his wallet and extracted a foil-wrapped packet. On the way over to the party, Johnny had offered him a condom from the stash he kept in his own wallet, reasoning that tonight might be the night Kees got lucky. Kees had laughed the offer away, never imagining that he might find himself with a hot stranger about to pluck his virginity.

He turned his gaze back to the wall while his companion sheathed himself. In moments, he felt that big body covering his own, and hot breath against his ear.

"That's it. Spread your arms and legs for me," the man murmured.

This is it, he thought. *No turning back now. Tonight, I become a man...*

His lover pushed his cock home. For a moment, Kees fought against the overwhelming pressure, but then he relaxed, and the thick length pushed inside. It filled him a fraction at a time, until he was skewered, pinned to the mattress like a butterfly in some museum exhibit. The man gave him a moment to get used to being so completely full, then he began to thrust—slowly at first, but then gathering pace. Fucking him, driving him to respond with full-throated gasps and grunts that vocalized his need.

The friction of his cock rubbing against the rough mattress was all it took to trigger his orgasm. He cried out as his cum spurted onto the fabric.

In response, his lover sped up even more, pounding Kees' arse hard now. In the moment before he came, he sank his teeth into the soft flesh of Kees' shoulder, leaving a mark that he would carry for days. Claiming him... He roared out his climax, then slumped on top of Kees, spent.

Kees lay for a moment in blissful abandon, feeling soporific warmth spread through his limbs. How sweet it would be to fall asleep in this man's arms and wake to the sight of his beautiful face. Then they both seemed to recall they were lying on a dirty old mattress in a squatters' residence and hauled themselves into a sitting position.

Already his companion was reaching for his shirt, slipping his arms into the sleeves and buttoning it hastily, as if he'd remembered he had somewhere else to be.

"That was fantastic," he said, stepping into his trousers, "but I have to go before anyone realizes I've been here with you."

"You can't leave, not like this," Kees said, all his euphoria blown away by the shock of being abandoned. "I mean, I don't even know your name."

"Oh, you'll learn it. Have no fear about that." But he made no attempt to enlighten Kees further. "You're special to me, Kees. Always believe that."

If I really am special, why are you walking away from me like this?

One concern still nagged at him, more important than anything else.

"Please…"

The stranger paused on the threshold to the room, in response to Kees' passionate entreaty.

"I need to know — Will I see you again?"

"When the time is right. You are meant to be mine, but only when you are ready to learn what I really am."

What kind of answer is that? Kees wanted to ask but just like that, the man who'd taken his virginity had gone. He struggled into his jeans and dashed barefoot out onto the landing, calling after him not to leave, but there was no sign of anyone. He had disappeared as surely as if he'd never been there.

Kees staggered back into the room, feeling utterly alone. From outside came the staccato clatter of firecrackers exploding and voices yelling, "*Gelukkig Nieuwjaar!*" Happy New Year. He looked at his watch, and realized it was a minute after midnight. Despite all Johnny's dire prophecies, when Kees looked out of the window, he could see no signs of widespread disaster, no burning buildings or crashing planes.

But with the man he'd fucked so passionately only moments before having walked out of his life without a backward glance, somehow it still felt like the end of the world.

Chapter One

The Present Day

Kees stared out of the plane window at the fields of North Holland, laid out in a neat patchwork beneath him. In a few minutes, they'd be landing at Schiphol, and he would set foot on Dutch soil for the first time in fifteen years. Part of him had thought he might never come back. When he'd packed his bags and left home, days after Millennium Eve—the night that had changed everything—he'd somehow known he was saying goodbye to his mother for the last time, even though he'd promised her he would come back and visit as soon as he was settled in London.

Less than two months later, before he'd even found his feet in his new home, his mother and his *oma* Annie were dead, killed in a gas explosion that had wrecked their apartment block. Numb with grief and shock, Kees hadn't even been able to face going back for the funeral.

In the intervening years, nothing had drawn him back to Amsterdam. He'd kept in touch with Johnny, not wanting to lose contact with his oldest and best friend. Though who would have thought life would turn out the way it had for either of them?

Johnny had gone down to see Tyler, the pierced guy from the squatters' party, and his band play at the Paradiso, and struck up a friendship with them. When their bass player had walked out in some row over 'creative differences', Johnny had auditioned to become his replacement. Fifteen years on, he was still a member of Chaos Theory, touring the world and regularly topping the rock charts. Kees had every one of the band's albums and on their last tour of the United States, he'd even gone backstage at their Madison Square Garden concert. When they'd met up after the gig, Johnny had asked him if he had any plans to go back to Amsterdam.

"Not as long as I'm needed in the office here," had been his emphatic reply. "After all, what's there for me any longer?"

It was a question he'd asked himself many times and when he did, his thoughts would inevitably drift to that golden-eyed stranger. After that fateful party, he'd pondered the guy's words over and over, wondering what he'd meant when he'd said Kees was meant to be his but only when the time was right. He could only conclude that he had been rejected due to his inexperience. So he'd gone away, first to London then to New York, to learn and grow, and become a man. He'd had lovers in that time, and every one had taught him something new about himself, whether they realized it or not, but there had never been anything to compare to that first, incredible time.

'You are meant to be mine.' The words were burned in his memory. Sometimes he thought he was stupid for holding onto that promise, to the thought that one day

they would be together again. *But if you'd really believed that would happen, you would have gone back to Amsterdam long ago, to find him and show him what you've become.* Still, he knew that for all he projected an air of self-assurance, deep down he was still the same uncertain, vulnerable boy standing alone while the party went on around him.

The distinct bump as the plane's wheels made contact with the runway brought Kees back to awareness of his surroundings.

"Ladies and gentlemen, welcome to Amsterdam," came the pilot's voice over the intercom. "The temperature here is eighteen degrees and overcast. You may now turn on electronic devices, but please do not unfasten your seatbelt until the plane has come to a complete halt at the terminal…"

Kees was one of the first off the plane, yet another of the perks of flying business class. The company had, of course, made the booking on his behalf, just as they'd found him suitable accommodation for the length of his stay here. Everything had to be in order for this job, the biggest of his career by far. They'd always had faith in his abilities to get to the bottom of any problem, and this was his opportunity to repay them.

Clearing passport control and collecting his luggage were formalities. Kees looked around him as he emerged into the arrivals hall, having been assured someone would be waiting to meet him. Sure enough, a man in a charcoal gray chauffeur's uniform, complete with peaked cap, stood holding a piece of paper on which was printed 'KEES VAN DER VEER'. He made his way over to the driver, wheeling his suitcase behind him.

The man smiled, and tipped the brim of his cap in greeting. "*Goedemiddag, Meneer* van der Veer. Did you have a pleasant flight?"

"I did, thank you, and please, call me Kees." It felt slightly strange to be talking in his native tongue again. Even when he'd met up with Johnny after the Chaos Theory concert, they'd found themselves speaking in English so as not to exclude the three Americans who made up the rest of the band from the conversation.

"Of course. May I take your case?"

"Oh, there's no need for that." Kees hated being fussed around, even though he knew the chauffeur was only doing his job. "Let's just get out of here."

He followed the man out through the arcade of shops that dominated the entrance hall of the airport, marveling at how the area had expanded in size while he'd been away. Dozens of self-service ticket machines had been erected by the front doors and at almost every one, passengers waited to buy tickets for train services to the center of Amsterdam and stations beyond. Kees and the chauffeur—whose name, he'd managed to discover was Rick—bypassed these queues, as well as the long line of people standing patiently at the taxi rank.

Rick's car, a sleek, black Mercedes, stood in the short-stay parking area close to the terminal entrance. He hefted the suitcase into the boot then came round to open the front passenger door for Kees.

"So, were you out of the country on business?" Rick asked, as he pulled the car out into the traffic waiting to join the motorway.

Kees shook his head. "This is the business trip, if you want to look at it like that. I work in New York."

"Now there's a city I've always wanted to visit. Been there long?"

"Thirteen years, almost. Before that, I was in London for a couple of years. This is the first time I've been home since." He glanced out of the car window at a collection of new-looking apartment blocks, screened off from the road by high fences. The bright, graffiti-like 'for sale' banners that adorned one of the blocks brought back irresistible memories of a dockside building that bore the slogan 'the soul of Amsterdam — not for sale' — memories of the events that had unfolded within its neglected walls. He shook his head, willing away thoughts of the night that had caused him to flee the city in search of something he'd never quite found.

If Rick wondered what had kept Kees away for so long, he didn't mention it. "Well, you won't find that things have changed too much — not in the heart of the city, at least. Though you must visit the Rijksmuseum. Since it had its facelift, it's really very impressive." He took his gaze off the road for a moment to flash Kees an apologetic grin. "Sorry, I'm talking like a tour guide now."

"Don't worry about it. I might well have time to fit in some sightseeing while I'm here, and I'm hoping to catch up with an old friend." The last email he'd received from Johnny had mentioned that Chaos Theory were back in Amsterdam, working on songs in preparation for recording a new album. It would be good to see him again, and spend some serious time together.

"Well, if you're looking for somewhere to have dinner one night, I know this fabulous little French restaurant in the Negen Straatjes. Everything's organic, and they have an amazing wine list..."

They talked companionably for the rest of the journey, Rick only slowing his flow of chatter when they reached the narrow, crowded roads in the city center and he had to keep his eye out for pedestrians stepping into his path.

The company had found Kees a top-floor apartment in a side street that connected the Herengracht and Keizersgracht, two of the major waterways that encircled the old heart of the city. It was located over a chemist's shop that still bore the traditional sign of the apothecary — a cartoonish representation of a Moorish face with a pill on its sticking-out tongue. *In other places, such a sign might well have been consigned to the history books — but not here.*

Rick offered to help Kees take his case up the narrow, vertiginous stairs, but he declined. The fare was on account, but he handed over a generous tip, thanking the chauffeur for an enjoyable journey. When the Mercedes had driven away, he stood on the pavement for a moment, taking in the sights that had once been so familiar to him — the constant flow of cyclists on rattling, black-framed bikes, pedestrians pausing to admire something that had caught their eye in a shop window, a glimpse of a pleasure boat making stately progress along the canal. Then he fished the key to the apartment from his jacket pocket, and went inside.

Whoever had chosen this place had done well. It had a bedroom, which looked down onto the street, a bathroom with both a shower stall and what appeared to be a whirlpool bath, a large living–cum–dining area with a small, open-plan kitchen area. The appliances were modern and a row of gleaming stainless steel pans hung over the stove. At the back of the apartment were French windows that let out onto a balcony big enough to hold a round wooden table and two matching chairs. It would be a pleasant place to have breakfast on sunny mornings, with a view over the walled back garden that had a small fishpond, and beyond that, the gardens of the grand houses on the adjacent Herengracht.

Checking his watch, Kees realized he had no time to stand and admire the view. Unpacking his suitcase would also have to wait. In less than fifteen minutes, he had an appointment at Excelsior Systems, the firm who was in need of his services. They were over on the Singel, not a great distance from here, but he wanted to arrive on time. It would never do to give this new client the impression that he couldn't be punctual.

He set off at a brisk pace, knowing he would have time later to walk these same streets at his leisure. Turning down a side street, he passed the restaurant Rick had mentioned and made a mental note to check out its menu. By necessity, he'd become a good cook in the years since he'd left home, but that didn't mean he didn't enjoy eating out whenever he had the opportunity.

Excelsior were located in what had once been one of the impressive merchants' homes that lined this particular stretch of canal, built in the years when the Netherlands had ruled the waves and Amsterdam's citizens had become wealthy by trading in spices. Now, like most of these buildings, it had been turned over to commercial interests. Kees had lost count of how many nameplates for doctors, lawyers and advertising agencies he'd seen fixed beside the front doors of these houses.

He pressed the buzzer for the entry phone. When it was answered, he said, "Hi, this is Kees van der Veer.

I have an appointment with Arjan de Wit at four-thirty."

"Ah, yes, *Meneer* van der Veer. Please come in."

The buzzer sounded and he was able to pull the door open. He walked into a cool, white-walled lobby. A young woman, her dark hair scraped into a bun and wearing a discreet microphone headset, smiled at him as he approached her desk.

"Take a seat, please. *Meneer* de Wit will call you through when he's ready."

A water cooler stood in the corner of the lobby. He pulled a plastic cup from the stack at the side of the cooler and helped himself to a drink. The receptionist was speaking to someone via her headset, and he had just settled himself in a seat when the receptionist announced, "If you'd like to go down the hall, it's the third door on the right."

"Thank you very much."

Kees tossed his empty cup into a convenient waste bin and walked down until he found the office with the name 'A DE WIT' stenciled on the door. He took a moment to straighten his tie and run a hand through his hair, hoping he didn't look too much like he'd just stepped off an eight-hour flight from New York.

In answer to his knock, a voice called, "Come in."

When he stepped into the office, he found himself face to face with a man he recognized all too well. A man with a wild mane of blond hair and strange, golden eyes.

Chapter Two

"Kees, it's good to see you again."

Kees was sure his mouth must be gaping as wide as that of the apothecary's sign, but he tamped down his surprise and answered the man with the steadiest voice he could manage. "You're Arjan de Wit?"

"At your service. Though I'm rather hoping you'll be at mine."

Damn the man. Kees had only been in this office a matter of seconds, and already Arjan's words were full of innuendo, though maybe his overheated imagination saw implication where none existed. After all, how many years had he spent dreaming of the moment when he'd finally encounter his lover from Millennium Eve once more? And now here he was, with so many unanswered questions buzzing around in his brain, and he couldn't find the voice to ask a single one.

"Please, do come and sit down." Arjan gestured to the empty chair at the opposite side of the desk to his own. With his shirtsleeves rolled up to his elbows and his tie fastened in a loose knot around his neck, he didn't appear to have aged a day since Kees had last seen him. He looked relaxed, in control and intensely sexy.

"I'll ask Karin to bring you through some coffee. How do you take it?"

"With milk, no sugar. Thank you."

Arjan picked up his phone, and spoke into it rapidly. Then he set the receiver down, regarding Kees with a steady gaze. "I'm pleased to see how well you've done for yourself, Kees. They tell me you're the best in the business at what you do."

"Oh, I don't know about that…" A flush rose to his cheeks. In all the years since he'd last seen this man and with all he'd achieved, he'd still never grown accustomed to receiving compliments.

"But you have a ninety-seven percent success rate. Those are impressive statistics, by anyone's reckoning." He paused in response to a knock, then called out, "One moment, Karin." He rose from behind his desk and went to open the door.

The receptionist who'd greeted Kees earlier walked into the room carrying a tray, on which stood two cups of coffee and a milk jug. She set one of the cups and the jug down before Kees. Arjan took the other cup from her. "Thanks, Karin. That'll be all."

Kees added a splash of milk to his drink, then took an experimental sip. Now, this was something he'd missed. No matter what other delights life in New York had to offer, and how much the Americans considered themselves connoisseurs of what they called 'joe', nowhere had he managed to find a blend as rich and deliciously bitter as the one he drank at this moment. Though the Dutch might no longer be the world power they once were, in his view they had no peers when it came to making coffee.

He set the cup down and looked at Arjan, who was back in his seat. "So, tell me what it is you need me to do."

"Are you familiar with the concept of electronic currency — more specifically, that of cryptocurrency?"

Kees nodded. "Of course," he replied. How strange it was that when it came to business he could talk so calmly to this man. After all, they shared a history that, however brief, had shaped the course of his life.

"It's a difficult concept for the average man to get his head round," Arjan went on. "The thought that, in effect, there is a form of currency that is effectively made up of pieces of digital information, encrypted so they can be traded securely. We are so used to thinking of money in terms of banknotes and coins that it's hard to conceive of it not existing in physical form. But those who propose its use are sure that one day it will consign those notes and coins to history, just as the euro made the guilder extinct."

"That's an interesting way of looking at it." Kees took another sip of his coffee, savoring the taste.

"I'm sure you can see why such a currency has its attractions. For one thing, it's not produced by any central agency or financial institution, meaning it's entirely free of government interference — no fixing of interest rates, and no hefty bank charges for transactions between one account holder and another."

"And no paper trail for someone wishing to launder money or hide the full extent of their income from the taxman," Kees pointed out.

"Exactly, which is why the world's governments aren't exactly fans of these new currencies, to put it mildly." Arjan grinned. His expression sobered almost immediately. "Not that I advocate trading outside the law, of course. No, my concerns have more to do with the fact that what makes this system so attractive to users also makes it vulnerable. We know that traditional accounts are at risk of being robbed, but if you're a victim of identity theft, or someone skims your credit card and clones it, your bank will be able to reimburse you. If your money only exists as information and someone hacks your account—or your system crashes and you haven't made a back-up—then it's gone for good."

"So where do I come into all this?"

"Excelsior specialize in looking for and closing vulnerabilities in computer systems. We do our best to make them harder for the average hacker to break into, though not necessarily impossible. You have some experience in those areas yourself, don't you, Kees?"

They had researched his background well. He would give them that. But it was no longer his area of expertise.

"And you'll be familiar with the many ways in which a system can be manipulated—the repeated denial-of-service requests that can take a website offline, the viruses and worms that are increasingly being used to lock computers and hold them to ransom. For months now, we've been working on ways to prevent this type of threat from being used to attack and destroy stores of cryptocurrency. But it's become ever more obvious that someone is distributing information about what we're doing to the hackers, enabling them to keep a step ahead of us all the time—and that someone can only be an employee of Excelsior. Kees, I need you to find out who's sabotaging our work."

Kees nodded. In recent years, he'd moved into the field of industrial espionage, rooting out all those who sought to bring down a company, whether by leaking secrets or bribing employees. This was not the first time he'd been asked to find someone who wanted to destroy a business from within.

"Do you have any suspicions? Anyone in particular you'd like me to investigate?"

"We only have a small number of our staff working on this project. It's one of those cases where the fewer people know what we're planning, the less chance there is of someone inadvertently leaking information. You don't expect that they might choose to leak it on purpose. After all, we look after our employees well here. The pay and perks are among the best in the industry. We've always believed that encourages loyalty, as well as rewarding hard work."

"So what's changed?" Kees set his empty cup back in its saucer and wondered whether the receptionist could be persuaded to bring him a refill.

"Who knows? Maybe someone just got greedy. All I know is that you need to find them, and soon, before they cause too much damage to our company's reputation, and to the safety of future cryptocurrency transactions."

Arjan paused, pushing his hair away from his face. Like so many things about the man, the gesture was seared into Kees' memory. Kees felt his cock swell in response and fought to temper his excitement. The reaction was so inappropriate in this business setting, but he simply couldn't help himself. Fifteen years and still his desire for this man had not faded. However much he'd tried to hate Arjan for seducing and abandoning him, his efforts had been in vain.

"Just tell me where to start, and I'll get straight on with my investigations." Kees hoped the slight strain in his voice was not apparent.

"I have names for you, though I'd rather not pass them on here." Arjan gave a rueful smile. "Call me paranoid, but I'm beginning to have doubts about the security of even my own office. And anyway, we have other things to discuss that have nothing to do with the matter at hand."

"We do?" Kees gave a nonchalant shrug, as if he didn't know what the man was talking about.

"I know it's been a long time, but I sense you still haven't forgiven me for walking away from you all those years ago. I'd like the chance to explain why I did it, tell you all the things you weren't ready to hear at the time." He got to his feet and took his jacket from where he'd draped it over his office chair. "If you're agreeable, I'd like to treat you to dinner."

It wasn't even five o'clock, far too early to be thinking about an evening meal, but Kees found his stomach rumbled in response to the suggestion. He'd eaten on the plane, but that seemed like an awfully long time ago now. "Thank you. That would be nice."

They left the office, and Arjan said his goodnights to the receptionist. "If anyone calls for me, Karin, tell them I'll get back to them tomorrow. Kees and I still have business to discuss."

"Of course, *meneer*. We'll see you in the morning."

Out on the street, Arjan strode off in confident fashion. Kees fell into step beside him.

"So, where are we going?" he asked. He thought of the restaurant he'd passed on the way to Excelsior. Somewhere like that would be ideal—a small, intimate spot, where they could talk without anyone intruding on their business.

"You'll see when we get there. I just need to know one thing, Kees. Are you a vegetarian?"

"No. To be honest, I'll pretty much eat anything that's put in front of me."

"Good. Not that I have anything against people who don't eat meat, but it's hard for me to have anything in common with them."

Again, Kees felt like Arjan had told him a joke whose punchline he failed to grasp.

They continued on, along the busy Raadhuisstraat, where traffic was backed up in the nearest Amsterdam ever came to a rush hour, and across the cobbled Westermarkt. Here, tourists waited for entry to the Anne Frank House, to visit the tiny attic rooms where the Frank family had hidden from the Nazis. When Kees had left for London, the house had just reopened after an extensive renovation that had turned it into a fully-fledged museum. He didn't remember the queues being as long then as the one that now stretched around the corner, into the marketplace before the grand Westerkerk.

The church bells rang out, signaling the quarter hour. The sound was another of the things Kees didn't realize he'd missed about the city until he experienced it again. Did Arjan pay any attention to the bells, he wondered, or were they something he took for granted — just part of the background noise?

"Not much farther now," Arjan commented, as they stepped into the road to bypass the busy entrance to the museum.

They traveled another block, then crossed over the pretty bridge that spanned the canal.

"Here we are…"

At first, Kees thought Arjan referred to the little bistro on the corner, the kind of venue the Dutch knew as an *eetcafé*, and appeared to specialize in tourist fare like steak and frites and chicken satay. It seemed appealing enough, though Kees couldn't see what might make it worth the walk, when they'd already passed three or four similar spots en route. However, Arjan went past it and stopped before the black-painted front door of one of the neighboring houses. He pulled a bunch of keys from his pocket then unlocked the door.

"Come in, Kees."

If the man had deliberately intended to wrong-foot him, he couldn't have done a better job. Kees had never expected that Arjan would take him to his own home. But he let himself be ushered inside, and climbed the three flights of stairs to Arjan's apartment.

"This is a nice place you have," Kees commented, once they were inside. It had much the same layout as the one he was staying in, though there appeared to be a second bedroom.

"Well, I could have found something closer to the office, but you can't beat the view out onto the canal. And there's a great little café just opposite here, on the Leliegracht. I like to go there for breakfast on Sunday mornings." As Arjan spoke, he shrugged out of his jacket before loosening his tie. "Can I get you something to drink, Kees? Beer? A glass of wine?"

"Beer would be fine, thank you."

Kees made himself comfortable on the sofa while Arjan went to fetch their drinks. He looked round the room, admiring the clean, Scandinavian lines of the furniture. A sleek flat-screen television hung on the wall directly opposite the sofa. Another wall was dominated by an abstract oil painting. Splashes of color in sunburst shades adorned the canvas, in contrast to the muted creams and grays of the room's color scheme.

Arjan returned with a couple of glasses of beer and handed one to Kees. "Try this. It's a pale ale, from a new brewery up on the Westerdok. I think you might like it."

Kees took a sip, finding it light and hoppy. "Yes, it's nice. Very refreshing."

Arjan set down his beer, then reached for his briefcase. He pulled out a tablet and swiped his finger over the screen. Having found whatever he'd been looking for on the computer, he handed it to Kees. "Here you are. A little something for you to read while I go and put the steaks on. How do you like yours?"

"Medium rare would be fine."

"Sure."

Kees looked at the document Arjan had pulled up for him. It contained details of the three Excelsior Systems employees who were assigned to the cryptocurrency project. Photos, résumés, details of their previous work within the company. He familiarized himself with their faces and names, knowing that if Arjan's suspicions were correct, one of them was responsible for the ongoing leak of information.

After what seemed like only a few moments, he heard Arjan calling to him. "The food is ready if you'd like to come through."

Kees closed the document he'd been reading, picked up his half-empty beer glass then strolled into the small dining area. Arjan had set two places for dinner and a candle burned on the table. Whatever the man intended to discuss in an atmosphere like this, it certainly didn't involve industrial espionage.

Without being told, Kees took a seat. Arjan had put out a plate of bread, and Kees helped himself to a slice before buttering it thickly. He couldn't recall the last time a client had invited him to their home for dinner, and he appreciated the novelty.

"I do like to see a man with a healthy appetite," Arjan commented, as he brought their food to the table.

Kees swallowed his mouthful of bread. "Sorry, I should have waited…"

"No, that's fine. Dig in. There's plenty to go round."

The steak had been cooked just the way Kees had requested. Pink and tender in the middle, it almost fell apart under the lightest pressure from his knife. He couldn't help noticing that Arjan's steak was so rare it was bloody and that the man devoured it with almost indecently quick bites.

Arjan had finished his beer, and he poured himself and Kees big glasses of rich, red wine, heavy with the taste of berries and old leather.

"So," he said at length, mopping up the juices from his plate with a hunk of bread, "I suppose there are a few things you want to ask me."

Only one. Why wasn't I good enough for you?

Chapter Three

Kees studied Arjan across the dinner table, trying to arrange his jumbled thoughts into some kind of order. He'd waited so long for this moment and now it had arrived, he didn't quite know where to begin.

"All I want is an explanation," he said at length. "After all, I've spent long enough waiting for one."

"Of course. Though I don't expect you believe what I'm about to tell you."

What the hell was that supposed to mean? Kees said nothing, just clutched the stem of his wine glass and regarded his companion through wary, narrowed eyes.

"Kees, the night of the party, I told you that you were mine—and I meant it. We are supposed to be together."

"Which is why you promptly walked away from me and we've spent the last fifteen years apart." Kees tried and failed to keep the bitterness out of his tone.

"We might have been reunited sooner, if you hadn't left the country. I would have come looking for you before now if I'd known where you were. Instead, I had to wait for fate to bring us back together."

"Fate?" It was a concept he wasn't sure he believed in. Johnny, on the other hand, was very firm on the subject. He'd always told Kees fate had taken him into the path of Chaos Theory, at the very time when they'd been in need of a new bass player. But then Johnny always had been the superstitious one.

"I need someone with a specialized set of skills to help me solve my problem. Is it just coincidence that you're the one who's acquired those skills?"

Kees drank his wine and waited to be convinced by Arjan's argument.

"More than that, I knew you were mine from the moment I walked into that party. Even above the smell of dope and body odor and old cooking oil, I was aware of your scent."

This was getting stranger by the moment. What did Arjan mean, *his scent*?

"It told me only one thing, Kees. You were the one I'd been searching for. My mate."

"I don't understand."

"Kees, I know this will be difficult for you to accept, but I am not human."

Kees snorted. "What are you talking about? You look human enough to me." Though even as he spoke, he knew Arjan's claim answered some of the questions he had. It explained the golden eyes, like those of a wild beast, the ravenous appetite and feral intensity of the man. But it still unsettled him.

"My people," Arjan went on, "are shifters. In certain circumstances, I have the ability to change my form into that of a lion."

Kees' mind immediately flashed to horror movies he'd seen, tales of werewolves and things that went bump in the night. "Oh, come on. You don't seriously expect me to believe that, do you?"

"You think I would joke about something like this?" Arjan's voice deepened, became more of a growl. When he looked up from his wine glass, something dangerous flashed in his eyes.

For a moment, Kees thought he saw the planes of the man's face alter, as if a beast really did lie beneath that handsome surface. He wanted to put it down to the alcohol, but he hadn't yet drunk enough. That glimpse of something he could only describe as 'other' made him more inclined to believe Arjan's story.

"So you're telling me you become a lion whenever there's a full moon?"

Arjan shook his head. "Our bodies don't move to that kind of cycle. It tends to be extremes of emotion that prompt us to shift, like when we're angry or afraid — or when we're on the hunt." He smiled, obviously noticing the shock on Kees' face. "Don't worry. You're not likely to see a lion prowling the city's streets any time soon. We're a little more discreet than that."

"You mentioned your people. How many of you are there?"

"Our pride numbers around two dozen. It's the largest in the Netherlands, but there are others of greater magnitude scattered around the world. And we have been here as long as Amsterdam has been a city, guarding our territory and keeping ourselves hidden from those who would wish to do us harm." He sloshed more wine into his glass before topping up Kees'. "Of course, life is much safer for us now than it was in previous centuries."

"And why's that?" Kees' curiosity was piqued. Inclined as he was to dismiss Arjan's claims, the man spoke with conviction and his story made a weird kind of sense.

"Our existence has been known of for a long time. And in a more superstitious age, the people of Amsterdam were mortally afraid of us, in the same way they feared witches and demons. They were convinced that we would come upon them in their beds and rip out their throats while they slept, and so they looked for someone who was prepared to hunt us down. They appointed a man who became known as De Jager—the Hunter—and with every successive generation, that role was passed on to the one most suited to the task. Always De Jager was chosen from among a handful of the oldest and wealthiest families in this city, the ones who saw us as the biggest threat to their comfortable, privileged way of life."

"This is incredible," Kees muttered. Arjan's words held him spellbound, and he'd stopped wondering how the story related to his own experience.

"But my people changed our ways to match the threat," Arjan continued. "Those who had been active members of society withdrew from public life or moved to a place where they believed they would be safe. And as time went on, the citizens of Amsterdam came to see us as less of a threat. They lost their own place of prominence in the world, overtaken by the twin powers of England and America, and eventually, they faced a greater danger to their way of life than anything a few shifters represented."

He didn't elaborate, but Kees' mind flashed to thoughts of Anne Frank and her family, confronted by an enemy who saw them as less than human, and the many other residents of the city who had suffered during the Second World War. In the face of invasion, widespread persecution and starvation, he could see how older, less immediate threats might recede into the background.

"And so, Kees, you would have grown up knowing of us only as some kind of bedtime story designed to frighten little children, if you were told of us at all. But since the Millennium, there has been a new tension in the city. A feeling that things have changed here, and not for the better. We started hearing that De Jager walks the streets of Amsterdam once more — that for the first time in more than a century, the families have convened and chosen a man to track us down. I would have dismissed this all as rumor and hearsay, if it wasn't for the fact that in the last few months a couple of pride members have been found dead in suspicious circumstances."

"And you think they were killed by this De Jager, whoever he is?"

Arjan nodded. "That's not the official story, but there is no other logical explanation. Whoever did it was clever. They made it look like Anneke had died from an overdose of heroin, but whatever else she took, I know she never touched that shit. Wim? Well, he had a heart attack that could have been explained by any number of reasons, but I'm convinced that was somehow drug-induced, too. He was a nice guy, but way too trusting..." His voice trailed off. "But you don't need to know about any of that. Not right now, anyway. I still haven't explained why I treated you the way I did."

"I always thought it was because I was too young for you. That you wanted someone with more experience, more knowledge of what it takes to please a man."

"Kees, those skills can be taught, and I would have had a lot of fun teaching you what I like. Though for your first time, you didn't do too badly, as I recall..."

The comment had Kees blushing. At once, his mind filled with images of a dimly lit room, the bass beat of music pounding up through the floorboards, and their two bodies, hot and covered in sweat, writhing together on a bare mattress.

"But you were right in one respect. At the time, I did have a problem with your age. Not because I was worried we might be breaking any laws but because as a shifter, my physiology is very different to yours. Our life span is around forty years longer than that of the average human, and we age much more slowly than you do. When we first met, I was already well into my thirties, and you were—what? Eighteen, right?"

Kees nodded. "And now…"

"I'll be fifty at the end of the month. And somehow, the years between us no longer seem to matter so much. I'm not proud of the way I behaved toward you, Kees. Never think that. But I did what I felt was right at the time. For both of us." Arjan swirled the wine around in his glass, looking at it rather than Kees. "Tell me… Would you have been able to cope with the truth of my nature if I'd revealed it then? And would you truly be the person you are today if we'd started a relationship that night?"

Kees took a long moment to consider both those questions. Everything he'd achieved, the successful career he'd carved out for himself… It all stemmed from his decision to leave Amsterdam. At last, he shook his head as something else occurred to him. "I might not even be alive today if you hadn't rejected me."

"How so?"

"My mother and grandmother died shortly after I moved to London. A gas heater in the apartment below theirs exploded in the middle of the night, while they slept. If I'd still been living with them, I would have been killed, too."

"I'm sorry to hear of your loss." Arjan looked grave. "But I hope now you understand that I never intended to hurt you. I only had your well-being at heart, Kees. And seeing you again, after all these years... Seeing the man you've become, I honestly believe I did the right thing."

"So what happens now?" Kees had become aware of a growing tension as they discussed their shared past. The feelings of hurt and regret were fading, replaced by an atmosphere he could only describe as sexual. He looked at Arjan's fingers, long and elegant, and wished they clutched his cock rather than the almost empty wine glass.

"Now?" When Arjan smiled, a hint of the beast within him seemed to emerge. "Well, I did plan for dessert. I have a nice butter cake in the kitchen that I picked up from a little bakery on the Keizersgracht. But, with your permission, I would very much like to take you to bed instead. Reacquaint myself with that gorgeous body of yours. Prove to you that all I have told you is true."

Kees knew he should refuse. Tomorrow, he would be starting work on the Excelsior project, and he ought to be getting back to his own apartment. After all, he hadn't as much as unpacked his case yet. Just like that first night with Arjan, things seemed to be moving a little too fast for him. Did the man really think that after fifteen years, a few words of apology, however heartfelt, could erase all the pain? All the nights of lying awake, wishing and wondering what might have been, if only things had worked out in a different fashion?

Yet he didn't make his excuses and reach for his jacket. He stood, pushing back his chair, and said, "I'll let you lead the way."

The neutral color scheme of the rest of the apartment extended to the master bedroom. A big, brass-framed bed was draped with a slate gray coverlet. Facing it, a plasma-screen TV had been fixed to the wall. Arjan didn't strike Kees as the type who would watch television in bed. But, he reflected, how much did he really know about this man? Enough to trust him, he supposed, as he sat on the edge of the mattress and kicked off his shoes.

Arjan came to join him, the springs sagging slightly beneath his weight, and they fell into an embrace. His mouth was warm against Kees', his kiss tasting of red wine. Their tongues tangled together, and Arjan gently guided Kees down so he was flat against the mattress, then lay on top of him.

The heavy pressure of that big body against Kees' took him right back to Millennium Eve and that feeling of rightness as Arjan had seduced him. Then, their coupling had been rushed, but now they had all the time in the world to touch and caress each other. Thick glazing on the windows kept noise from the street outside to a minimum, and Arjan's bedroom seemed to Kees like an oasis of tranquility, where nothing was able to intrude on their private time together.

Arjan worked on Kees' shirtfront with assured fingers. Each time another button came open, he kissed the skin he'd revealed. Kees was more than happy to lie back and be undressed, lust and alcohol making him loose-limbed and chilled out.

Once Arjan had undone Kees' shirt entirely, he sat up and removed his own shirt. His broad chest was covered with blond curls that reminded Kees irresistibly of a lion's sandy pelt. Could it really be true that his lover had the ability to change into animal form? It seemed so unlikely, yet looking at Arjan, with his flowing hair and powerful, muscular frame, the idea did not seem so much of a stretch.

Then Arjan reached for Kees' belt, and as he began to remove it, Kees could think about nothing but the sensations of being stripped down to his skin.

Having been undressed, he sprawled back against the pillows to watch Arjan get naked. He took his own cock in his hand, and Arjan purred, "No touching, Kees. Not until I say so."

It seemed they had fallen into the same roles as that night at the party, with Arjan setting the pace and Kees more than happy to respond to his commands. He realized it was what he had missed in the years they had been apart—a man with that sense of natural authority, who would issue instructions and expect them to be obeyed. Kees didn't think of himself as submissive, but something deep in his soul responded to Arjan's dominant aura. There had to be a pecking order in the pride, he assumed, and Kees wondered where Arjan fitted in. Or had his lover's desire for other males precluded him from taking his rightful place at the top of the pack?

Arjan came forward, his dick rising from the wild mass of hair at his groin. The invitation was too much to resist. Kees got onto his hands and knees, then shuffled along the bed till the two of them were almost touching. He gripped Arjan's shaft by the base, holding it steady so he could drop a loving kiss on its tip.

"You want this?" Kees looked up into those strange golden eyes. "Want me to suck you?"

Arjan's lips curved in a smirk that would have been arrogant on any other man. *He knows who's really in control here.*

Kees bent his head and took Arjan's cock into his mouth. His lover's sharp musk filled his nostrils and he breathed in deeply. Everything about this man was perfect, from the way he tasted to the way his domed crown felt as it butted against the inside of his cheek. Arjan was right. They were meant to be together.

He sucked hard, using all the little tricks he'd been taught in the years they'd been apart. If anything drew a particularly urgent response, he repeated it. When he'd last been with Arjan, his experience had been nil. Now, Kees wanted to show him all he'd learned.

When he took Arjan's balls in his hand and caressed them, Arjan gave a soft growl that couldn't help but remind Kees of a cat's purr. He trailed a finger down the seam between them, all the way to the tight pucker of Arjan's arse.

Pulling his mouth off his lover's shaft, he said, "Oh, you like that, don't you? You're just a big pussycat who likes to be scritched…"

"Don't you ever call me that," Arjan roared, though there was no real malice in his words. Grabbing both Kees' wrists in one strong hand, he wrestled him onto his back, though in truth Kees made no real efforts to escape.

Being manhandled in this fashion sent a fresh jolt of excitement surging to the root of Kees' dick, and he moaned. He found himself lying with his head resting on the very edge of the mattress, and his arms hanging down toward the floor.

"Now, swallow me," Arjan ordered. He maneuvered himself so that his cockhead was pressed to Kees' lips.

Obediently, Kees opened his mouth and let Arjan push himself inside. In this position, all Kees could do was relax his throat and allow his lover to fuck it with slow, careful strokes. He breathed through his nose, feeling the soft curls at Arjan's groin tickle his skin.

He was preparing himself for the flood of cum that would surely fill his mouth at any moment when Arjan pulled out, and rolled him onto his stomach. None of his other lovers had possessed a fraction of Arjan's more-than-human strength, and being thrown about the bed turned him on beyond belief.

Kees heard, rather than saw, Arjan fit the condom. A dollop of something cool and sticky landed with unerring accuracy against his arsehole, and he sighed as Arjan worked the lube inside him. As soon as he was loose and relaxed, Arjan guided him up onto all fours and climbed on top of him. Gripping Kees around the waist with one hand, he used the other to help him slide home. Inch by inch, he pushed steadily deeper. Kees pushed back at him, bearing down, allowing him even further inside.

Arjan's thrusts grew harder, faster, the frame of the bed creaking and shaking. With each stroke, he let out a feral grunt, his breath harsh and hot in Kees' ear. Reaching beneath their two bodies, Kees took hold of his own cock and began to wank it with frantic tugs.

"Oh, Arjan," he groaned. "I need to come so badly..." He didn't quite know why he felt the need to seek permission for his orgasm.

By now, Arjan appeared to have gone beyond words. His only response was a strange, guttural noise, low in his throat. The knowledge that the beast in his lover was so close to the surface frightened and excited Kees in equal measures. He gave his shaft a final squeeze as hot semen arced into the air. In that same moment, the jerking motions of Arjan's hips stilled. He clutched Kees tight, and Kees knew his lover had reached his own peak.

Arjan slowly eased himself out of Kees' arse, and they shared a soft kiss.

"Let me just go and dispose of this…" Arjan's voice faded as he padded out of the room.

Tears pricked at the corners of Kees' eyes and he swiped them away, stunned by the depth of emotion he felt. He'd thought he might never experience the feeling of being with Arjan's again and now here he was. What they had shared had surpassed all his expectations, all his dreams. Now Arjan had found him again. Kees hoped he would never let him go.

"Move over, lazybones."

Kees looked up to see that Arjan had returned and shifted on the bed so he could join him, careful to avoid the wet patch on the sheet. Once they were comfortably entwined, Arjan pulled the covers over both of them. Resting his head on his lover's chest, listening to the slow, steady beat of his heart, Kees began the slow drift into sleep.

Chapter Four

Arjan lay staring at the blade of pearly dawn light that sliced through a crack in the curtains. Beside him, Kees dozed, his hair mussed on the pillow, and the little crease between his eyebrows smoothed out by sleep. He looked so young, so in need of care and protection...

Filled with restless energy, Arjan fought the desire to pace the room. Every fiber in his body yearned to shift, to give his inner lion free rein. He'd experienced the same feeling when he and Kees had been fucking, roused by the heat of passion generated between them.

That urge had been there from the moment he'd first become aware of Kees, fifteen years ago. He hadn't even been thinking of meeting his mate that night, but he'd gone out on the balcony of the dockside apartment he was renting and caught the young man's scent on the wind. Faint as it was, it had compelled him to follow his nose and blag his way into a party he hadn't even known was taking place. Among all the other smells in that squalid warehouse, Kees' unique aroma had stood out, spicy and distinctive, like the top note in a perfume designed for Arjan alone.

He'd always thought he would find his mate in one of the prides scattered across the Netherlands, and the shock of realizing Kees was human had been overwhelming. It had been difficult enough for the members of his pride to accept that Arjan was attracted to other males. Forming a relationship with Kees could see him cast out altogether. But that scent. It clouded his reason, made him forget all sensible considerations...

Seeing Kees standing uncertain and alone, clutching his drink so tightly that he threatened to crush the little waxed paper cup, had done nothing to diminish Arjan's certainty that they were intended to be together. The boy had been beautiful, with that mass of brown curls and the dimple in the point of his chin. But he'd been younger than Arjan had expected, not yet out of his teens, and with so much still to learn about himself. The right man, at the wrong time.

All these years later, that home in the Eastern Docks was a distant memory. Along with glittering success in his career had come a level of pay that enabled him to buy this apartment. The squatters had been driven from the last of the dockside warehouses, and the laws had been changed to prevent them taking possession of such properties in future. A few still defiantly occupied a handful of graffiti-covered buildings on the Nieuwezijds Voorburgwal that had become something of a tourist attraction, but he had no doubt they would eventually be forced to leave those, too. Things changed. People moved on, whether they wanted to or not—just as Kees had done.

He had no regrets about what he'd done that night. Kees had been ready for him, despite his inexperience, and their bodies had melded, become one. And tonight, they had recaptured that same heat of passion. It had never been as good, or as intense, with anyone else.

It said something for the strength of their bond that the young man hadn't fled the apartment once he'd learned the truth of Arjan's nature. No, Kees was stronger than that. But was he strong enough to face all the challenges that might lie ahead of him?

Arjan got out of bed and walked through to the living room naked, needing to be in a more open space. They hadn't bothered to clear away the dinner plates before going into the bedroom, and he caught a faint, lingering scent of red meat that made his mouth water. All his appetites were greater than those of a human, and sometimes he found it hard to hang onto the veneer of civilization, when all he wanted to do was tear at a piece of raw beef with his strong incisors or plunge his cock over and over into a lover's tight arse...

Arjan could hold back no longer. He closed his eyes, relishing the sensation as he shifted from man to lion, sinking down onto all fours as his arms and legs became sturdy, fur-covered limbs. The thick carpet tickled the velvet pads of his paws, and he threw his head back and shook his mane. If he had been out in the wild, he would have roared, announcing his presence and calling others in the pride to join him, but he retained enough of his basic human nature to know that making enough noise to wake his neighbors in the small hours was never a wise idea.

For a moment, he let himself do nothing more than exist, freeing his mind of all the clutter that had prevented him from returning to sleep. When he opened his eyes, Kees stood in the doorway, silhouetted against the light that came from the bedroom.

"What the—?" The young man's expression was a mixture of horror and awe.

He could do nothing to explain, not in his lion form. Hastily, Arjan shifted back, experiencing sharp twinges of pain as his joints realigned themselves and his spine straightened out. Rising from his crouching position, he could only mutter, "Kees?"

"I woke up and you weren't there," Kees explained. "I was thirsty, so I came through to get myself a glass of water and saw…" His voice trailed off. Clearly, he was struggling to articulate just what he had seen.

"Come sit with me," Arjan said, walking over to the couch. "We should probably discuss this."

"What is there to discuss? I mean, you told me you're part lion, and that you can change your shape. I just didn't expect to walk into your living room and see the proof."

"Kees, I know this must come as a shock to you, but I didn't intend you to see me like that. Not tonight, anyway. Only when I judged you were ready for it."

"You seem to know an awful lot about what I'm ready for, don't you? You say you're taking my feelings into account, but really it's all about looking after yourself."

"That is not true." His voice rose in volume, and the urge to shift came upon him again—to assert his dominance in this, his own territory. But Kees was his mate, the one he swore to protect and care for above all others, and that made his home Kees' territory, too. Speaking more calmly, he continued, "I told you I have a tendency to shift when my emotions are roused, and no one affects me the way you do, Kees. If I didn't care about you and if making love with you didn't touch a place in my soul that no one else has ever come near to, then this wouldn't have happened. It's a battle to keep my animal nature under control — one I don't always win."

Kees wrapped his arms around himself. "I'm sorry. Maybe I overreacted."

Arjan shook his head. "Anyone would have felt the way you did. Not that any of my previous lovers had any idea I was anything other than a regular guy." He paused, thinking back to all the men who had come before — and since — Kees, and why he had never needed to have this conversation with them. "I've never been with anyone from within my own pride or any other, for that matter. So few of us are naturally attracted to our own sex that opportunities are limited, as I'm sure you can imagine."

"But your parents... They're okay with what you are and that your boyfriends are human?"

"They fear for me, but don't all mothers worry about what their children get up to?" He gave a rueful smile. "But they have always done their best to support me, even if they don't ask to know the details. And they know that I would never do anything, be with anyone who I thought might prove a danger to the pride." He got to his feet. "Let me get you that glass of water, Kees, and then you can go back to bed."

"Thank you."

Arjan found two glasses from the cupboard above the kitchen counter and filled both of them with bottled water from the fridge. He walked over to where Kees still hovered on the threshold of the room and handed one to him. He drained his own glass with a couple of quick, gulping swallows. Until that moment, he hadn't realized quite how thirsty he was.

"I'll probably have left for work when you wake," he told Kees, "but feel free to sleep as late as you want. Take a shower. There are clean towels on the rack under the washbasin in the bathroom, and I'll leave out a toothbrush for you."

"Don't you need me to come into the office with you?"

"Not tomorrow. I want you to spend time making yourself thoroughly familiar with the background of this project. You have the files with all the details of the three main players. I need you to look at the work each of them has done, see if you can find any clues there as to who leaked that information."

"Sure." Kees nodded, sounding more assured now they had moved on to a more neutral topic. "Leave it with me." He cast a hopeful look in Arjan's direction. "Are you coming back to bed?"

"There's not really any point. I doubt I'll sleep now and anyway, I need to be in the office early. I have a conference call with a client in Berlin. And you need some time to yourself. But I'll ring you. We'll have dinner tonight."

With a little resigned shrug, Kees wandered back to the bedroom. Arjan collected his white terrycloth robe from where it hung on the bathroom door, slipped it on, then went to make a pot of coffee.

Mug in hand, he settled down on the sofa and tuned the television to a channel showing the local news. A reporter stood before the Royal Palace in Dam Square, discussing an impending visit from the Danish head of state. Arjan let the images flow by without really seeing them, and hoped that Kees would understand why he needed to keep this small but necessary distance between the two of them.

* * * *

The street was quiet as Arjan let himself out of the house on the Prinsengracht. On the opposite side of the canal, refuse collectors were throwing bags of rubbish into the back of their truck and the occasional pedestrian passed by on their way to work. He always enjoyed this time of day, before the city had properly woken up. The tourists were still in their hotel rooms, the late-night revelers sleeping off their excesses and the children had not yet begun their noisy procession to school.

Yet this morning he did not have the sense of ease and well-being he'd expected, given the mind-blowing sex he'd enjoyed last night. As he passed the looming tower of the Westerkerk, he could not shake the feeling that someone was watching him from the shadows, waiting for the perfect moment to pounce.

Arjan gave himself a mental shake. *Don't be foolish. You're in no danger here. It's just those stories you told Kees haunting you.*

Still, he couldn't dismiss the threat of De Jager out of hand. The man had killed twice already and would do so again unless he was caught. But if he tried to strike, Arjan would be ready for him. He wasn't like Anneke or Wim, vulnerable and easy to manipulate. He was stronger than any foe, and knowing that he had an enemy gave him the advantage. It meant that part of him was always on the alert, quick to respond to any threat.

His real concern was Kees. He didn't know whether his lover had fully grasped the danger he had placed himself in, simply by getting involved with Arjan. But they were meant to be together, and no outside threat would be allowed to encroach on their happiness. He would make sure of that, whatever it took.

Arjan looked around with a defiant glare, as if daring anyone to threaten him and the people he held dear. Let them try, and he would make them regret it.

Chapter Five

Kees stood in the shower, lathering himself up with the grapefruit-scented gel he'd found on the bathroom shelf. Arjan had told him to help himself to whatever he needed. He couldn't help wishing that the big man was here now, pressed up against him under the steamy spray.

It had been gone ten by the time he'd woken, his jetlagged body catching up on much-needed sleep. Arjan, of course, had left for work hours ago. Kees had thought about sending him a text then decided against it. That seemed too unprofessional, too needy.

Anyway, Arjan had been right. He did need time to himself. He had to get back to his apartment, unpack and make a trip to the nearest supermarket to stock up with milk, coffee and all the other essentials. More immediately, he needed breakfast.

As he toweled himself dry, he remembered Arjan mentioning the café on the Leliegracht. This seemed like as good a time as any to try it out.

He dressed and left the flat, making sure the door shut securely behind him. A young man was sitting on the steps that led up to the building, a cup of coffee in one hand and a cigarette in the other. He nodded at Kees in greeting. Kees assumed he lived in an apartment on one of the other floors. With gardens at a premium, most of the residents of Amsterdam made the most of any outdoor space they had, whether that was a balcony or just their own doorstep.

Kees crossed over the canal and found the café. Half a dozen tables were arranged on the small stretch of terrace before it, but he bypassed those and went in search of a seat inside. He found a space at the big wooden table by the front window, on which the morning's newspapers were scattered.

A waitress with a candy-pink stripe in her hair came over to take his order. He glanced briefly at the menu before settling on an *uitsmijter*, that savory combination of fried eggs, melted cheese and ham he'd never found anywhere outside the Netherlands.

"And a glass of orange juice and a cup of tea," he added.

"Sure," the girl replied, scribbling his order on a pad before walking over to the counter.

He picked up that day's copy of *Het Parool*, and turned to the sports pages. Even after all these years away, he still kept an eye out for Ajax's results, even managing to catch the odd game on the big screen at a sports bar he frequented on the Lower East Side. The main headline told him that Manchester United was interested in signing the team's promising young left-back. He skimmed the rest of the story, only looking up when the waitress returned with a glass mug of hot water and a wooden box containing a variety of tea bags.

Kees made his choice — English Breakfast — and the girl took the box away. He dunked the tea bag in the mug and watched the liquid swirl. His thoughts drifted and for the first time he allowed himself to consider what he'd seen when he'd walked into Arjan's living room in the early hours.

If he closed his eyes, he could still see that big, shaggy-maned lion standing in the middle of the floor, swishing its tail in menacing fashion and regarding him with an unblinking, golden gaze. At first, he'd thought he was still dreaming, but the animal had been too real, too solid. Its strong, feral scent had permeated the air and though he'd wanted to move, fear had held him rooted to the point.

And then... Had he really watched the lion transform back into the naked figure of Arjan? It seemed impossible to believe, but he knew his eyes hadn't deceived him. The process had been swifter than he'd expected, and he was sure it must have caused Arjan some serious discomfort, judging by the grimace on the man's face. But it had happened, and somehow he'd managed to take it in his stride, as if it was a regular occurrence with all his lovers.

"Here you are." The waitress broke his reverie by placing his breakfast in front of him.

"*Dank je wel.*" Having thanked her, he reached for the orange juice. He took a big gulp, then started tucking into the *uitsmijter*. Kees broke into a smile as he registered the distinct flavor of mustard cheese — something else he'd never been able to find on his travels. Though that, he had to admit, was probably for a good reason. It was definitely an acquired taste, like raw herring, and the sickly yellow advocaat his grandmother used to drink on festive occasions.

At a table to his left, an elderly couple were poring over a map, and talking to each other in rapid French. A sleek black cat strutted across the floor and out to find the sunniest spot on the café terrace. Kees paused with his fork halfway to his mouth to watch its progress. The animal carried itself with the same assurance he'd seen from Arjan—or, rather, the lion that Arjan had become.

But if he accepted that Arjan was part of some extended family of lion shifters that had lived in this city for centuries, he also had to accept that those shifters were being tracked down by a man who had been engaged to kill them. In that case, not only was Arjan's life at risk, his own could be, too. Kees didn't want to think about that, not when the world was carrying on all around him and everyone from the pink-haired waitress to the French tourists were oblivious to the secrets he had learned last night. He'd been engaged to root out a threat of a very different kind—the saboteur who threatened the security of Excelsior Systems' latest project. That, not some mythical hunter who might not even exist, had to be his focus in the coming days.

* * * *

It was another couple of hours before Kees could finally sit down and concentrate on the mole in Arjan's data management team. Once he'd finished his breakfast, he'd gone back to his apartment and set about unpacking. Then he'd visited the supermarket and stocked up on everything he thought he might need, from fruit and cheese to a couple of bottles of good red wine. He had also thrown a box of condoms and a bottle of lube into the shopping cart, just in case he found himself entertaining Arjan. It never did to be unprepared.

Now, at last, he was able to curl up on the sofa, a mug of coffee on the table before him, and set to work.

He read through the detailed files on each of the suspects in turn. Thijs Kempen, Rob van Bergen and Eline Vos. All three were in their early twenties and had been recruited by Excelsior on graduating from university. They were talented, ambitious, hardworking and apparently popular with their colleagues, yet one of them was committed to bringing down the cryptocurrency project.

Kees struggled to find an obvious reason why any of the three would choose to undermine their own work. He knew the motives behind this type of behavior were as varied as the reasons given for hacking into a system. Some wanted to expose a security flaw in the program, some were in it for the money they could make, while others did it simply because they could.

Spending time with the members of the team would help him make a better assessment of their personalities, but it would be difficult to find some way of meeting them without arousing their suspicions. He also needed access to the computers they used in the office, so he could discover whether files had been deleted, overwritten or otherwise tampered with.

When he told people what he did for a living, most assumed that he routinely placed bugs in phones and keyloggers on computer equipment, so he could keep tabs on everything a suspect did. Usually, this led to a lengthy explanation of the legal minefield surrounding such a course of action. In order for any prosecution to succeed, Kees had to make sure that— as far as was humanly possible—his activities remained within the law. Additionally, in this particular case, he was dealing with members of staff who were far more computer-savvy than the average office worker and would know how to look for any spyware installed on their systems if their suspicions were aroused.

As he read on, Kees jotted down notes on a lined shorthand pad, detailing the questions he would need to ask Arjan when they next discussed the issue. He needed to know whether any of the team worked odd hours and not only because they might be conducting their nefarious activity when they were alone and unobserved. If he could spend a few hours in the office undisturbed, that would give him time to start running the necessary diagnostics.

When his phone rang and he glanced at the display, he was surprised to discover it was almost five o'clock. He'd been so engrossed in his work, the afternoon had slipped by without him realizing.

"Kees, it's Arjan. I hope I haven't disturbed you."

"Not at all. I'm way overdue a break." He stretched, easing out a crick in his neck. "Been hard at work reading those files you gave me and I have to say, I feel like I'm looking at three model employees here."

"I know. That's what makes this so hard to take. I look at Thijs, Rob and Eline and I really can't believe that one of them would want to damage the company so badly. But that's not why I called. I just wanted to let you know that I've made us a reservation for dinner. Seven o'clock, at Kristof's on Reestraat."

That gave him plenty of time to change into something more formal than the T-shirt and jogging bottoms he currently wore. "Sounds good. Shall I see you there?"

"Yes. I'd like to have met you earlier, but I'm in meetings till six-thirty."

"You work far too hard," Kees chided him.

Arjan chuckled. "It's how you become the boss. *Tot later*, Kees."

"Yeah, see you later," Kees echoed as the call ended. He didn't put his phone down immediately. Instead, he scrolled down his contact list till he found a number he hadn't rung in a very long time.

The ring tone sounded for so long, Kees expected the call to go to voicemail. But at last, a familiar voice said, "Johnny Dekkers."

"Johnny, it's Kees."

"Hey, man, good to hear from you." Johnny sounded as cheerful as ever. "How are things in the Big Apple?"

"I wouldn't know. I'm in Amsterdam right now."

"Seriously? Since when?"

Kees rose from the sofa and walked over to the window, so he could look down on the street below him. A couple of men sat chatting on the front step of the building opposite, and a woman was trying to persuade her little terrier not to sniff at something of interest it had found in the gutter. "I got in yesterday. I'm going to be around for a couple of weeks or so, working for a company on the Singel. I just wondered whether you'd be free to meet up."

"Are you kidding? Like I couldn't find time for my best friend? How does Saturday afternoon suit you? You can come over and see my place. We've got some heavy-duty catching up to do..."

"That would be great. I'll bring beer."

He made a note of the address and said his goodbyes to Johnny, then went to change. After all, though Arjan hadn't said as much, he had a hot date to get ready for.

Chapter Six

Sometimes, life gives you a lucky break. For the first time since he'd agreed to help find the saboteur within Excelsior Systems, Kees found himself on the receiving end of a slice of good fortune that left him smiling. He'd received a call from Arjan to say that Thijs Kempen had managed to upend a bottle of iced tea over the keyboard of his company laptop. Thijs had been issued with a replacement, but instead of the damaged piece of hardware being sent to Tech Support for repair, it was now with Kees. It meant he had undisturbed access to any secrets that might have been deliberately concealed.

The machine had taken a frustratingly long time to dry out, but now he was able to search for deleted files. The software he used had provided a breakthrough in another case he'd worked on. It had proved that a senior administrator within the firm had been systematically getting rid of important data. Even though the man had gone to significant lengths to cover his tracks, Kees had eventually been able to recover much of that data. He had also run the deletion program the administrator had used on another computer, producing results that showed exactly how he'd operated.

Now, however, as he munched on a cheese and salami roll and studied the results of his forensic work, he was beginning to believe the young software engineer was not the company mole. There was evidence that Thijs had got rid of various files, but these appeared to be nothing more sinister than a handful of personal emails. Kees hadn't discussed with Arjan Excelsior's policy on employees using computers for anything other than business matters. But only the hardest-hearted of bosses would see the messages Thijs had sent—making plans for dinner with his girlfriend or arranging to meet his friends at some club or other—as a dismissible offense.

So, one down, two to go. But even though it would have resolved a lot of problems if he'd found the culprit at the first attempt, a small part of him rejoiced at the thought that he would need to spend more time on the case. More time in Amsterdam, with Arjan.

Recalling Arjan's suspicions about the security of his office phone, Kees contacted him by text message instead.

As far as I can see, Kempen is clean. Will need to be given access to the other two computers ASAP.

Then he rang Thijs' direct line. "Hi, this is Tech Support. I've got good news. We've managed to salvage the information on your laptop."

"Thanks." The young man sounded genuinely grateful.

Kees wondered how much of a chewing-out he'd received for spilling liquid on the machine. He was about to tell Thijs that he'd be bringing the computer back to the office when he heard a woman spitting out curse words in the background.

"Hey!" Thijs' voice was muffled, as though he'd placed his hand over the phone's mouthpiece. "Keep it down, will you?"

"What's going on?" Kees kept the inquiry casual.

"Oh, it's Eline, fighting with her boyfriend on the phone again. He's probably trying to scam money out of her with another of his sob stories. Rob and I keep telling her the guy's a loser, but she won't listen to us..."

When Kees put the phone down, he made a mental note to see if he could find out more about Eline Vos' relationship. She wouldn't be the first person he'd ever investigated who had a partner with money problems, and that had certainly been a motive for selling information in past cases. The sooner he could get his hands on her computer—and that of Rob van Bergen—the happier he would be.

Assuring himself that he'd done all he could for the time being, Kees powered down the laptop. It was still early afternoon, but over the years he'd become used to working odd hours, often spending all night running some diagnostic program or other and catching up on his sleep during the day. He'd made no plans to meet Arjan tonight, not knowing how long it might take him to work through everything on Thijs' computer. Dinner would be pasta and homemade carbonara sauce, one of his never-fail recipes, more than likely eaten in front of the television. There was a selection of DVDs on a shelf in the living room, mostly American films Kees had already seen, subtitled in Dutch.

He thought about turning on the TV, but decided against it. Instead, he closed his eyes and let his mind drift where it would. Inevitably, his thoughts turned to Arjan.

The man sat behind his desk, having called Kees into his office to give him the results of his investigation into Thijs Kempen. As ever, Arjan looked handsome in his Italian-designed suit. He fiddled with his platinum cufflinks and waited for Kees to speak.

"I'm afraid it's bad news. I've turned up nothing that would indicate Thijs is the one who's passing on information to an outside source."

"Oh well, I suppose it was too much to hope that you'd be successful at the first attempt. But that doesn't mean you're entirely absolved from punishment."

"What are you talking about?"

Kees wriggled on the sofa, making himself more comfortable against the cushions. Almost without being aware of it, he had pushed a hand under the waistband of his sweatpants so he could grasp his cock. His private fantasies often took a turn in which a man chastised him for some or other misdemeanor. Given Arjan's naturally dominant bearing, it was really no surprise that Kees should imagine his lover as a cruel but tender disciplinarian.

"Those are the rules, Kees." Arjan was clearly reveling in placing him on the back foot. "Did I not explain them to you before you began your investigations?" He stood, then took off his jacket and hung it neatly on the back of his chair. Then he came round from behind the desk. As he continued speaking, he undid those stylish cufflinks before rolling up his shirtsleeves to reveal his brawny forearms. "You find the person responsible for stealing data relating to the cryptocurrency project as speedily as possible or you suffer the consequences."

"But I'm trying. Now I know I can exclude Thijs. It'll be easier to concentrate on the other two..."

"I don't want excuses. I want results. What part of that don't you comprehend?"

"I'm sorry, meneer." 'Sir'. What else could he call him under the circumstances? With that simple word, he knew he was ceding all control in this situation. He stood with his hands behind his back as Arjan slowly paced round behind him.

"So, now that you understand my position, I'm sure you will appreciate that although I regret what I have to do to you, it's both justified and necessary." When Arjan spoke, his breath was hot against Kees' neck.

"Yes, sir." Kees was all too aware of the heavy pressure in his groin as blood flowed to his dick, making it swell. Harder than he could ever remember being, he needed relief – and soon – but he knew Arjan would not permit him that luxury.

"Take down your trousers and underwear, Kees. And hurry to it."

"But – " He could hear voices coming from the other side of the office door as people passed by in the corridor. Uncomfortably reminded they were not alone, he stammered, "The door. Aren't – aren't you going to lock it? What if someone comes in?"

"Then I'll invite them to stay and enjoy the view. Don't tell me you have objections to that."

He wanted to protest, to say that he didn't deserve any of this. But he knew that he would consent to whatever indignities Arjan might choose to inflict on him, knowing the shame and humiliation he suffered would make the coming pleasure all the sweeter.

Under Arjan's intense gaze, Kees stripped from the waist down, making a neat pile of his shoes, socks, combat pants and undershorts. The hem of his T-shirt brushed against the tops of his thighs. The fabric tented out by the strength of his erection. He felt deeply foolish but even more aroused.

He half expected to be told to bend over the desk. Instead, Arjan said, "Reach down and grab hold of your ankles."

In this new position, he could not help but feel exposed, the T-shirt riding up his back to display his bare arse cheeks.

"Don't worry, as this is your first offense, the punishment won't be too severe. Just six swats. I'm sure you'll be able to take those without making any noise, won't you, Kees?"

He wondered what would happen if he failed to endure the spanking in silence. Would Arjan increase the number of smacks, or would he fling open the door and invite the whole office to witness Kees' embarrassment? This being fantasyland, he was free to imagine any number of possible outcomes, each more outrageous than the last.

Arjan didn't bother to warm him up. This wasn't the prelude to a long punishment session, after all. He brought his strong palm down sharply on Kees' right cheek, driving the breath from him with the force of the blow. A second slap followed almost immediately, this time on his left cheek. Pain blossomed and spread throughout his arse and when Arjan repeated his actions, right…then left again, Kees had to call on every drop of his self-control not to hop from foot to foot and beg the man to stop.

A final two swats – if anything, even harder than the previous ones – rounded off the promised half dozen. The fire in his arse still burned, but behind the ache followed a growing feeling of pleasure, as endorphins kicked in.

"Very good. Now stand upright," Arjan commanded.

As he let go of his ankles, Kees realized he'd been clutching them so tightly his fingers had left pale imprints in the skin. His head swam, and he thought tears might spring to his eyes. But, just as he'd been instructed, he bit his lip and refused to let even the smallest whimper escape. Arjan had to be proud of him for that.

"Very good." For the first time, there was a note of admiration in Arjan's voice. *"It seems my boy is as strong as I'd hoped. And because you took your punishment in silence, I'm going to allow you a reward. I'm going to let you bring yourself off."*

Obediently, Kees wrapped his fingers round the base of his dick. With long, slow strokes, he worked them up to the head and back, collecting the moisture he found there on his fingertips and using it to lubricate his flesh. This was about putting on a show for Arjan, letting him enjoy the sight of Kees jerking off.

Bringing his other hand down to cup his own balls, he let out a low sigh. He felt no guilt about playing with himself. Who knew better than he did just where and how he liked to be touched, how much pressure he liked applied to the sensitive spot where crown met shaft?

All too soon, the need to come overwhelmed him. Arjan regarded him in silence, a satisfied smile quirking his lips as Kees lost his battle to hold on, and milky white seed erupted from the tip of his cock.

He lay sprawled on the sofa, panting and vaguely aware of the need to find some tissues to mop up the cum that had puddled on his belly. If fantasizing about being spanked by Arjan was that good, how much better, he wondered, could the reality be?

Chapter Seven

After a couple of days when they had been able to spend almost no time together, Kees sat in the lobby of Excelsior Systems, waiting for Arjan's last meeting of the day to end so they could go to dinner.

At last, he was able to put down the newspaper he'd been listlessly reading, as Arjan walked over to the front desk in company with a bald, bespectacled man in a pinstriped suit. The two shook hands and said their goodbyes, the visitor promising that he would get his secretary to email over the necessary documents. Then Arjan turned his attention to Kees.

"Hey, hope I didn't keep you waiting too long."

"Not at all, but I am ready for a beer and something to eat."

"Okay, well, let's go. Karin," Arjan addressed his receptionist, "if anyone from Tricom calls, tell them I'm on the case and they'll hear from me in the morning."

"Of course, *Meneer* de Wit. And have a pleasant evening, both of you."

As they left the building, Kees noticed a young dishwater blonde standing on the pavement smoking a cigarette. She was pretty but a little too thin, with the washed-out look of someone who spent all day in a room that received little natural light. He recognized her from the personnel files Arjan had given him.

"That's Eline Vos, isn't it?"

Arjan nodded. "I'm surprised she's leaving so early. The last couple of weeks she's been here till at least seven every night. I tell all her team not to work so hard, but with the pressure of having to stay one step ahead of the opposition…"

As they watched, Eline stubbed out her cigarette and went to embrace the man who'd just joined her.

Must be the boyfriend. Kees scrutinized the new arrival. He wore a khaki army-style jacket, had a triangular black scarf knotted loosely around his neck, and his hair was matted into dreadlocks.

The young man dropped a kiss on the top of Eline's head and wrapped an arm around her as they walked off down the street. Kees heard her laugh in response to something he'd said. From their body language, they gave no indication of the trouble in paradise Thijs Kempen had described. Was he right to consider that Eline might be leaking information, or should he be digging into the background of her work colleague, Rob?

As if he'd read Kees' mind, Arjan said, "By the way, you'll have unrestricted access to those computers you need to examine soon enough."

"Really?" Kees' expression brightened. "How did you swing that?"

"It's King's Day at the end of the month. Everyone gets time off—apart from you, unfortunately. I hope you don't mind."

He shrugged. In his years away from the Netherlands, Kees had almost forgotten about one of the country's biggest national holidays, held to mark the official birthday of the reigning monarch. While Amsterdam became a sea of orange, its citizens enjoying street parties and canal parades in honor of King Willem-Alexander, he knew he'd be hard at work, searching for the secrets either Eline or Rob had concealed on their laptops.

"I don't mind at all. But I'm getting to choose where we have dinner tonight, okay?"

Arjan acquiesced to his demand. Kees took them to a small, first-floor café in a building close to the Begijnhof — the enclosed group of almshouses that had once been a refuge for women who had taken a vow of religious chastity. The café had been one of his favorite haunts when he used to go out with Johnny and their other college friends, popular with students and tourists on a budget, thanks to its generous portions and very reasonable prices.

The room was crowded, but they found a table in a corner, away from the TV screens showing some Champions League football game. They ordered a couple of bottles of strong Belgian beer, and chatted about everything and nothing till their food arrived, accompanied by another round of drinks.

The beauty of this place is that everyone's too busy having a good time to pay you any attention. It was just as well given the way Arjan, still in his elegant work suit and silk tie, had eschewed cutlery in favor of eating with his hands. He gnawed every scrap of meat from the lamb cutlets he'd ordered and Kees was sure that if they hadn't been in public, he'd have crunched the marrow from the bones, too.

Soon, they were heading back to Kees' apartment, making their way through the red-light district, which was thronged with tourists at this time on a Friday night. Lingerie-clad women sat in the lighted windows, some announcing their availability by gyrating up against the glass, while others sat more decorously on stools.

They turned a corner, onto a quieter side street. Even here, sex was for sale, and the occasional window had its curtain pulled tight across, indicating that its occupant was entertaining a client.

As they passed the Café de Tulpen — another familiar local landmark — a voice boomed out from one of the pavement tables. "Hey, Arjan, my boy! Fancy seeing you here."

Arjan went over to hug the speaker, who had risen from his seat. "Uncle Danny, I didn't realize you were back."

"Yes, we just got into the city last night."

The two broke their embrace and Kees got a proper look at Arjan's uncle. He suppressed a small gasp of recognition. Danny de Wit. The man had been a permanent fixture on Dutch TV for as long as Kees could remember. He'd made his name as a singer and variety performer, before going on to host the top-rated game show, *Spin the Wheel*. Though his features were rounder and more florid than Arjan's and his eyes a soft hazel rather than that striking amber-gold, the family resemblance was all too clear. The entertainer must have been in show business for a good four decades now but he had the smooth skin and unlined complexion of a man half his age. Either he'd employed the services of a very skilled cosmetic surgeon or he shared the same strange shifter metabolism that made Arjan look so much younger than he was.

"Would you care to join us? Lise and I were just enjoying a nightcap."

For the first time, Kees noticed the woman who sat at Danny's table, an elegant blonde whose face was half-hidden behind a pair of oversized sunglasses. Was she someone famous too, Kees wondered. It would explain her attempts to hide her appearance.

Arjan glanced at Kees. "Why not? Uncle Danny, this is Kees. He's helping me with that business I was telling you about."

"Ah, yes." Danny extended a big paw of a hand, and gripped Kees' fingers tightly. "Lovely to meet you, Kees. What can I get you boys to drink?"

"Oh, just a coffee for me, please," Kees replied.

"And the same for me, thanks." Arjan took a seat at the side of his uncle, and gestured to Kees to sit.

Danny caught the eye of the waitress who had just brought an order to the neighboring table. "Two coffees when you're ready, sweetheart. And I'll have another cognac. Lise, my love, anything more for you?"

Lise shook her head. "I'm fine with this, darling." She gestured to the half-full glass of white wine in front of her. Her voice held an accent Kees couldn't quite place.

"So, Kees" — Danny spoke in the smooth, warming tone designed to make the contestants on his show feel at ease — "is this your first time in Amsterdam?"

Why did everyone keep asking him that? "No, I was born and brought up here, but I moved away when I was eighteen. This will sound strange, but I'd forgotten what a beautiful city this is."

"Finest in the world, I always say." Danny leaned forward in his seat to make his point. "Built on the principles of civic pride, the right to freedom of expression, and knowing how to have a damn good time, eh, Arjan?"

"So you tell me, Uncle." Arjan had the expression of a man who'd heard this same sentiment expressed many times before. "But how was Stockholm?"

"Oh, you know..." He waved a hand airily. He seemed about to add something else, but was interrupted by the arrival of the waitress with their drinks order.

"We stayed with my parents for a few days," Lise explained, as Danny took a long swallow from his cognac glass. "And then we took a cruise up to the Arctic Circle to see the Northern Lights. They were truly breathtaking. Even stunned my husband here into silence, for once." She gave Danny an affectionate pat on the arm, her gesture telling Kees all about the depth of emotion between the couple.

Kees could contribute little to the conversation, as Danny and Arjan caught up on family matters, swapping gossip about people he knew he would probably never meet. But he was happy to sit and enjoy the warmth of the evening, watching the passing parade on the street and letting the city's relaxed ambience permeate his soul. He'd meant what he'd said. He truly had forgotten about Amsterdam's beauty, so caught up in looking for a new home that he'd neglected everything his old one had to offer.

Even the sudden, raucous laughter of a hen party couldn't ruin his mellow mood. Dressed in matching pink T-shirts and with the bride-to-be carrying an inflatable male sex doll under her arms, the group had almost passed their table before one of them turned back, and smiled at Danny de Wit.

"Hey, you're the guy from *Spin the Wheel!*" she exclaimed. "I love that show. Can we have our picture taken with you?"

Danny stood up, smiling good-naturedly, and put his arm round the bride as the rest of the girls arranged themselves into a tight, giggling group. One of them handed a camera to Arjan, so he could take a couple of photographs.

Kees marveled at how Danny treated his fans. He knew he would have hated the intrusion on his private time, but this man clearly loved being the focus of so much attention. Having shared a few words with the hens, Danny gave each of them a peck on the cheek before they went on their way.

"You've made their night," Arjan commented, as his uncle sat back down.

"All part of the service." Danny grinned, then drained the last of his cognac. He looked over at Lise, who appeared used to strangers fawning all over her husband. "It's getting late, and I have a meeting with my agent at nine. Arjan, Kees, I'm afraid we're going to have to love you and leave you."

"That's okay. We should be on our way, too," Arjan said.

"We're going up to the taxi rank at the Nieuwmarkt if you'd like to share a cab," Lise suggested.

Arjan shook his head. "Thanks, but it's a nice night. We'll walk."

"Well, lovely seeing you," Danny said, "and you must come over for dinner one night. You, too, Kees. You work in computers, right? You can look at mine, and find out why it crashes every time I try to turn on my webcam." He clapped Kees on the back. "I'm joking, of course, but please, we'd be happy to have you over any time." With that, he gave a cursory glance to look for approaching traffic and stepped into the road.

The car seemed to appear out of nowhere, traveling fast and with music blaring from its speaker system. If anything, instead of the driver slowing down when he realized he was about to hit Danny, it looked to Kees like he actually speeded up. Kees had no time to yell out a warning to Danny to get out of the way. He heard a sickening crunch as metal hit bone and a high-pitched scream that came from Lise.

Danny de Wit was tossed in the air, to land in a broken, bloodied heap on the asphalt. He didn't move again—and the vehicle didn't stop. By the time anyone could react, the dark saloon was a faint shape in the distance.

"What the—?" Arjan was the first to find his voice. He dashed into the road and bent to run a hand on the side of his uncle's neck. "There's a pulse," he said urgently. "It's faint, but it's there. Someone call an ambulance."

People had emerged from the café's interior. Its proprietor, a young, dark-haired man with a long white apron tied around his waist, was among them. "What happened?" he asked, his expression turning to one of shock as he saw Danny lying in the street.

"He—he was hit by a car." Kees found he was shaking as he relived the moment of impact in his mind.

"Fuck, that's Danny, isn't it?" From the familiar way he spoke the name, it was all too clear to Kees that Danny de Wit must be a much-loved regular at the café. The barman went to join Arjan, undoing his apron as he went. He bundled it up and placed it carefully under Danny's head, attempting to make the injured man more comfortable.

Kees dialed one-one-two on his phone, the direct line to the emergency services. When the call was answered, he said, "I need an ambulance. A man's been run over... We're just off the Oudezijds Achterburgwal, by the Café de Tulpen... Yes, as soon as you can. He's really badly hurt..."

"Don't worry, *meneer*. The ambulance is on its way, and we'll be sending a police car, too. They'll be with you very soon."

The brisk tone of the dispatcher reassured him a little. *Please let him be okay*, he repeated to himself. *Please don't let him die.*

His thoughts turned to Danny's wife, and he turned to see how she was bearing up. She sat at the table, her face buried in her hands.

"Lise..."

She looked up at the sound of her name. Her dark glasses lay on the table and her eyes, paler gold in hue than those of Arjan, but no less striking, shone with tears. If he had not already come to suspect that Lise was another shifter, those eyes would have revealed her true provenance to him.

"Hey, it's going to be okay," Kees assured her. He went to sit beside Lise, throwing an arm awkwardly around her.

She clung to him, sobbing into his shoulder, while he did his best to soothe her. Arjan still knelt by his uncle, gripping the man's hand tight. A crowd of bystanders had begun to build on the pavement, gawping at the scene, despite the barman's best efforts to persuade them to move on.

Within a few minutes, the blaring of sirens attracted Kees' attention, and he turned to see the flashing lights of a squat yellow ambulance. The vehicle pulled to a halt and a male nurse, clad in the distinctive uniform of fluorescent yellow and blue jacket along with blue trousers, jumped down from the cab. He dashed over to where Danny lay, and began to check the man's vital signs.

In the wake of the ambulance came a silver saloon car, from which a tall woman in a plaid shirt over a white T-shirt and jeans emerged. Her dark hair was pulled into a low ponytail and she wore no makeup. She stood in the middle of the road, surveying the scene.

"Hey, Lise," Kees said, "the ambulance has arrived. Danny'll be on his way to hospital soon…"

Before he could offer her any more words of reassurance, he was stopped by a roar of pain and grief. When he turned to discover its source, he saw that Arjan had his face raised to the sky, the tears that glistened on his cheeks all too visible. The nurse, who had been joined by the driver of the ambulance, was shaking his head slowly. Kees didn't need to hear what the man said to know that Danny had lost his fight for life.

"No." Lise, too, seemed to have realized the implication of the nurse's gesture. "Please, God, no. Not my Danny…" She lapsed into her native Swedish, howling out words that Kees could not understand as she leaped from her seat and ran over to her husband's body.

The dark-haired woman looked round, as if wondering who best to approach to make sense of the chaotic scene. She walked over to Kees and flashed a police badge at him.

"I'm Inspector Sofie Engelen." She fixed him with a direct gaze. "Can you tell me what happened here?"

Kees tried to put his scrambled thoughts into some kind of order. "I—I was here with my friend." He gestured in the direction of Arjan, who stood watching as Danny's body was placed on a gurney and loaded into the ambulance. "We'd been having a drink with *Meneer* de Wit and his wife, and we were just saying our goodbyes to them. Danny stepped out into the road, and this car came speeding toward us. He—he didn't stand a chance…"

"What do you remember about the car? Color, make?"

"Dark blue…black, maybe. Local registration plates, I think, but I couldn't give you the number. I'm sorry, Inspector. It all happened so quickly."

"That's all right. We'll be talking to as many of these people as we can. Someone may well have seen something useful."

She nodded in the direction of the gaggle of onlookers. Most of them had drifted away now the initial incident was over, but a few remained, waiting to see what would happen next. To Kees' horror, they were clearly getting a rush from being on the scene of a crime involving someone famous. One or two even aimed their phones at the ambulance as it pulled away from the curb. He wouldn't be surprised if some of the footage they were filming ended up on tomorrow morning's news.

"All I know is that whoever was driving," he said, "it seemed like they wanted to hurt Danny."

"Now what in the world would make you say that?"

"Well, they didn't make any attempt to avoid him."

"From what you said, it sounds like they might not have been able to…not if he walked into the road right in front of them."

"In that case, surely they would have stopped when they realized what they'd done?"

"Oh, you'd expect them to"—her tone was dry—"but hit and run accidents are not exactly unusual. The driver panics, flees the scene..."

"There wasn't any panic here," Kees told her. "Just a weird kind of focus."

"And what? You saw that on the driver's face?"

"I didn't see the driver," he admitted. "But you have to believe me. This was deliberate."

"Is everything okay here, Kees?" Arjan had materialized at his elbow without him being aware of it. The tenor of his voice and his stance seemed deeply protective of the younger man.

"And you are...?" Her tone was sharp. Kees gained the impression this woman would not put up with having her authority questioned.

"Arjan de Wit. Danny is...was...my uncle."

The policewoman introduced herself, then launched into an interrogation of Arjan. "You and Danny de Wit were close?"

Arjan nodded. "Though I hadn't seen him for a couple of months. He and his wife had been on holiday in Sweden and before that, of course, he'd been busy filming his TV show. We just ran into the couple tonight. We'd been making plans to visit them for dinner..." He shook his head sadly, as if realizing that would never happen.

"Your friend seems to think that *Meneer* de Wit was deliberately targeted by the driver, that this was some kind of...assassination," Inspector Engelen said. "Did your uncle have any enemies that you know of?"

"Not a one," Arjan said firmly. "You're from Amsterdam, right, Inspector?" When the woman nodded in reply, he went on, "Then you'll know just how popular my uncle was. Talk to the barman of this place. I bet he'll tell you that Danny de Wit never once had to buy his own drink."

"Hey, Sofie, what have I missed?" The man who interrupted the conversation sounded breathless, as though he'd run to the scene from somewhere nearby. Reddish-blond hair brushed the collar of his denim jacket and a small diamond stud glittered in his left earlobe. Kees thought the guy looked more like the proprietor of one of the coffee shops where tourists went to smoke dope than a police officer, though he supposed that might come in useful in the course of undercover work.

Kees waited for a formal introduction to the man. It was not forthcoming.

"Piet." Inspector Engelen shrugged, as though all too used to the man's tardiness. "Where have you been? You weren't answering your radio."

"Following up a report of shots being fired outside a jeweler's near the Vondelpark. Turned out to be just some kids letting off firecrackers." He shrugged, as if to say 'what can you do?' "Anyway, I'm here now."

"Well, I need you to go over to the hospital, speak to de Wit's widow. See if she remembers anything about this car that hit her husband."

"Sure thing, boss lady." Before he turned to go, he let out a low whistle. "Who'd have thought it? Danny de Wit, of all people."

Inspector Engelen shrugged in non-committal fashion. She appeared to be the only person Kees had seen tonight who was not in awe of Danny's fame.

"As for you," she addressed both of them, "we'll be in touch. We still need to take a full statement from you. And don't worry, *Meneer* de Wit, we'll do everything we can to find the car that hit your uncle."

"Good. For a moment, I thought you and your colleague weren't taking this incident seriously."

"Well, I can see how you might reach that assumption. Piet may come across as way too casual, but he's one of the best detectives on the force. The problem is that because of who your uncle was, there'll be a lot of pressure on us to clear this case up, and I don't like working with that kind of burden on my shoulders. As I see it, all victims deserve to be treated with care and attention, not just the famous ones."

"Well, thank you for your candor, Inspector," Arjan replied, his face tight with suppressed anger. "And I look forward to speaking with you again. Now, if you don't object, I need to go and let my family know what's happened."

Kees took long strides after Arjan as he strode away. He grabbed the larger man by the arm, as if he might shake some sense into him. "Hey, the detectives are only trying to do their job."

Arjan came to a halt. His eyes were red-rimmed. Something deep inside Kees melted at the sight of his lover, always so controlled in his public emotions, in such obvious distress.

"You're right, Kees, I know that, but even if the woman does have some problem with her superiors, that doesn't mean she can take it out on us." He sighed. "I'm sorry. I just can't stop thinking about Danny lying there in the road, broken. And Lise... She was so in love with him..."

For the first time, Kees noticed the dark red stains that marred the front of Arjan's shirt. Blood must have been transferred there when he'd been cradling his dying uncle in his arms.

"Come on, Arjan. Let me take you home. We'll find somewhere we can pick up some brandy on the way. I think we're both going to need it."

The big shifter nodded and wrapped an arm around Kees' shoulders. "We shan't let him win, Kees," he murmured.

Him? Kees wondered, but Arjan said no more on the subject as they walked away.

Chapter Eight

Kees sat on the balcony, staring out into the darkness and sipping brandy. In the kitchen, Arjan was on the phone to his father, breaking the news of Danny's death.

The night held little warmth and he shivered, wondering if he should go back inside. He had come out here in order to give Arjan some privacy. He'd wanted his lover to spend his first night in the apartment in happier circumstances, but that had been before the accident.

Faintly, he could hear Arjan talking in a low, urgent voice, but managed to blank out the words. The combination of raw hurt and righteous anger that emanated from the man was painful to be around. Moreover, it reminded him all too sharply of the phone call he'd received to let him know his own mother and grandmother were dead. Nothing would ever erase the shock of such news.

At last, Arjan popped his head out through the French doors. He held a brandy glass in one hand and the bottle of Armagnac in the other. Kees couldn't help but notice that the level of the alcohol had gone down considerably since he'd topped up his own drink.

"Everything okay?" Kees asked.

Arjan lowered himself heavily into the available chair and placed the bottle on the table. "My father's not taking it too well. He and Danny were as close as brothers can be. And I really don't think he appreciates the truth of the situation. No, that's not quite right. He doesn't *want* to appreciate it."

"And what is that truth?"

"Danny's death wasn't some random hit-and-run accident. The driver of that car—it was De Jager," Arjan said. "I have no doubt of it."

"How can you be so sure?" Kees asked.

"Like I told that detective, there was no one else in this city who wished Danny harm. You saw how he was with those girls back at the café—he loved his public and they loved him. Go into any bar in the back streets of the Jordaan, and you'll find a photo of him with the owners. As soon as they release the news of his death, someone will start campaigning to build a monument to him. The TV stations will be repeating all those variety specials he filmed over the years. He was a local icon." His expression darkened. "That's what Inspector Engelen meant when she talked about the pressure she'll be under to solve the case. And it's what also got him killed."

"What, because he was famous?"

"I know. I know, it sounds crazy." Arjan rubbed his eyes, the strain of everything that had occurred in the last few hours etched on his face. "But Danny had the highest profile of all of us. He was the most visible. It was bound to make him a target sooner or later."

Arjan finished the last of his brandy, reached out toward the bottle to refill his glass then appeared to decide that getting any drunker than he already was would not be the solution to his problems. He let his hand drop into his lap.

"Until now, De Jager has been picking off the weakest among us," he said. "Anneke and Wim, they were both vulnerable people. It shouldn't have been a surprise that someone sought to do them harm. Anneke fell in with a bad crowd, stopped listening to her parents' advice, and Wim? Well, he would have given you the shirt off his own back if you were in need of it, but someone will always take advantage of that kind of generosity…"

Kees recalled what he'd been told about the girl who'd died from what Arjan believed to be a staged drug overdose and the man whose heart attack might have had a sinister cause. He wanted to dismiss his lover's claims as some crackpot theory, brought on by grief, but he couldn't shake from his mind the image of that car, accelerating toward Danny de Wit, from his mind.

"We've become far too complacent," Arjan went on. "Maybe we needed a wake-up call, to remind us what happens when we make ourselves too conspicuous. But why did this have to happen to Danny?"

Kees didn't like the tone of despair in Arjan's voice. "So you don't think this De Jager will stop now he's made his point?"

"He won't stop till every single one of us is dead. That's his sworn mission, as it has been since the families got together and appointed the first hunter. The members of our pride look out for each other, but there are always those who choose to walk a solitary path. De Jager must know that, and he'll be tracking them down."

"Hey" — Kees laid a reassuring hand on Arjan's arm — "these guys have been trying to wipe out the pride for centuries, right? They haven't succeeded so far, so who says they're going to do it this time? All you have to do is find him before he finds you."

"Maybe you're right, Kees. There's much to be done. We need to convene a meeting of the pride, work out what we can do to catch this bastard before he comes after another of us. My father might be too old and too set in his ways to think of a radical plan of action, but he knows that I am prepared to take whatever steps are necessary to keep us safe." Arjan growled out the last few words.

To Kees, it seemed that the beast lurking within Arjan would break through at any moment. The restless energy his lover exuded was all too palpable. He pictured himself sharing the limited space on the balcony with a wild, snarling lion and knew he had to calm Arjan down before that happened.

"You can think about that tomorrow," he soothed. "Come on, let's go to bed."

They took their glasses and the half-empty Armagnac bottle back inside, then set them on the kitchen counter before heading for the bedroom.

Kees had intended to do nothing more than curl up alongside Arjan and fall asleep, letting his lover have the reassurance that came from feeling another heart beating in time with his own, but Arjan seemed to need more in the way of comfort.

At first, Kees simply ran his hand over Arjan's back in slow, soothing circles, the way a mother might soothe a tired a fractious child. Then he remembered the massage bar that lurked in his wash bag. His last boyfriend, who'd turned out to be nothing more than a three-week fling, had bought it for him at a store selling handmade cosmetics in Greenwich Village. He'd intended them to use it together, but they'd split up before that had been able to happen.

"I'll be right back." Kees hauled himself off the bed and padded into the bathroom to retrieve it.

When he returned, Arjan was propped up on one elbow, the bedsheet draped in a thin line across his crotch. It had the result of making him look even more enticing than if he'd been lying there naked.

"What is that?" Arjan asked, as Kees began to rub the bar between his hands, releasing its essential oils and letting the scent of sandalwood and ylang ylang fill the small bedroom. The makers claimed the fragrance would act as an aphrodisiac. Whether that was true or not, Kees wasn't sure, but as an aid to good sex, it could only add an extra something.

"It's designed for sensuous massage," he explained. "Now, I just want you to roll over and enjoy."

Arjan did as he'd been told, allowing Kees to knead his shoulders. Hard knots of tension had gathered there, and Kees used the pads of his thumbs to break them down.

"Mmm, that feels good." Arjan's voice was muffled by the pillow.

"Well, it's soon going to feel a lot better."

Kees gradually worked his hands lower, gliding the palms over Arjan's lower back with gentle, sweeping motions. He had no real expertise when it came to massage, but he knew enough to keep from applying any pressure to Arjan's spine. Instead, he concentrated his attentions on the shifter's arse cheeks, squeezing the firm globes and feeling his own cock rise in response to the pleasure he was giving.

Arjan lifted his head, half turning it so he could address Kees over his shoulder. "God," he groaned. "My dick's so hard it's going to bore a hole through the mattress if I don't do something about it."

The graphic description almost sent Kees into a fit of giggles that threatened to derail the sensual mood he'd been trying his best to create. He pulled himself together enough to respond, "Well, we'll have to do something about that, won't we?"

He reached down, slid a hand underneath Arjan's belly to where his rigid length was trapped between the bulk of his body and the mattress, and touched it with his oil-slick fingers.

"Oh, yes..." Arjan raised his hips slightly, allowing Kees to make better contact.

The next thing he knew, they were rolling over, so each lay on their side, gazing into the other's eyes. Arjan reached for the massage bar, which Kees had left lying on the pillow, and rubbed it between his big palms. Then he wrapped his hand around Kees' shaft.

There was only one way in which this could end. The oils in the massage bar would cause any condoms they used to perish, unless they showered before sex. And while soaping each other up might have been fun, Kees was already so keyed up he knew he'd probably come while he was under the spray.

He wanked Arjan while his lover did the same to him, taking every opportunity to share long, deep kisses while they stroked their hands up and down each other's cock. Kees traced one of the fingers on his free hand around and over Arjan's arsehole, hearing the breath catch in his lover's throat in response. He grazed that sensitive place with his fingernail once more, delighting in the way Arjan writhed and whimpered, clearly loving to be teased like this.

Arjan humped his hips, pushing his shaft hard into Kees' slippery, encircling fingers. At the same time, he continued to shuttle his fist along the full length of Kees' dick. But he was clearly too excited to delay his orgasm any longer, and only a few moments later, his cum was shooting out and dripping down the back of Kees' hand.

Spurred on by the sight and sound of his lover roaring out his climax, Kees reached his own peak, hot jets of pleasure shooting through him. They clung together, Arjan pressing a light kiss to the hollow of Kees' throat.

"Thank you for being here when I needed you," Arjan murmured.

"What else could I do?" Kees replied. "You mean so much to me, Arjan. Never doubt that."

Arjan said nothing, just gave a satisfied little grunt and pulled the covers around them both.

Drifting off to sleep, Kees was jolted back to full wakefulness as a thought struck him. "Arjan, they'll have to do an autopsy on your uncle, won't they?"

Arjan made a noise in his throat that suggested he was not happy at being roused. "Why do you ask?"

"Well, what if they examine him, test his DNA or something, and they discover he's not human? What happens then?"

"Frankly, it's not very likely. The cause of his death isn't an issue—they know it was a car accident, and one that was witnessed by close to a dozen people. The pathologist will simply be looking for evidence of where the car struck him. If..." He paused, and swallowed hard, clearly struggling to express himself. "If they have to open him up, then all they'll think is that Danny was a remarkably well-preserved man for his age—or, rather, the age people believed him to be."

"Yeah, and I suppose if they were going to find anything amiss, they'd have done it when Wim or Anneke died..."

"Can we talk about this in the morning?" Arjan sounded impatient, as if he'd said all he was prepared to on the subject.

Kees realized he might have pushed his lover too far with his line of questioning. After all, he'd have felt uncomfortable if someone had started asking him about the circumstances of his family's deaths.

Tomorrow morning, before he went over to Johnny's, he would pay a visit to the cemetery and lay flowers on his mother's grave. The act should have been much higher on his agenda, given his failure to attend her funeral. But everything that had happened since he'd been reunited with Arjan had pushed it to the back of his mind. Now, it was time to make amends.

Kees went to murmur words of apology for raking over unhappy ground, but Arjan was already asleep.

Chapter Nine

The van der Veer burial plot was in the De Nieuwe Noorder cemetery, on the north side of the city. For Kees, getting there meant taking a bus from the Centraal Station out to an unprepossessing shopping center on the Buikslotermeerplein, then a short walk through the steadily falling rain. When he'd said where he was going, Arjan had offered to accompany him. But as comforting as it would have been to have his lover by his side, he needed to do this alone.

The cemetery had been opened in the 1930s and a collection of low, plain-looking stone buildings greeted him at the main entrance. Kees walked down a tree-lined gravel path, searching for the family grave. He hadn't been to this place in the best part of two decades, having visited a couple of times after his father had been buried here, and he had forgotten the aura of quiet calm that clung to it.

Again, he felt a pang of guilt at missing the funeral of his mother and grandmother. The arrangements had been made by his mother's only other living relative, a cousin, Jan, who lived in Haarlem. Jan had been the one who'd called Kees to let him know about the explosion. Though Kees had been listed as the official next of kin, he'd made it clear he would not be coming back to Amsterdam to sort things out. Now, he was a little ashamed he'd left those duties to a virtual stranger.

He walked on, past an eclectic collection of graves. Unlike many of the city's other cemeteries, this was for people of all religious beliefs, as well as atheists, and that was reflected in the items that adorned the various burial plots, from teddy bears to figures of Buddha. It seemed everyone had their own special way of remembering the ones they loved.

At last, Kees found the discreet headstone that bore the names of his father, his mother and his *oma* Annie. Under the rules of the de Nieuwe Noorder, only three people could be buried in any one family grave, for an initial term of twenty years. When that term expired — and that would be happening to this particular plot in less than three years, he realized with a jolt — it could be extended for anywhere from five years up to a maximum of another two decades. After that, the bones would be moved to the cemetery's central ossuary, to make room for other residents.

It was a more practical, less sentimental approach to death than Kees had witnessed in other countries. He'd visited Highgate cemetery when he'd been living in London, at the suggestion of some long-ago boyfriend with left-leaning views who'd wanted to pay homage to the grave of Karl Marx. Nothing here could compare to the magnificent statues and ornate mausoleums he'd admired there. There were no monuments designed to stand throughout the centuries. Nothing was forever, this site seemed to say. We left, and others took our place. That was the way of the world.

Kees dropped to a crouch and swiped away wet leaves from the grave so he could arrange the bunch of red roses he'd brought. They'd always been his mother's favorites. Though he was not a religious man, he looked to the heavens and issued a silent prayer.

"Mama, I'm sorry I couldn't have been a better son," he murmured. "I was too selfish, too headstrong. There are so many things I wish I could have said to you, and now I'll never have the chance. Forgive me."

Behind him, he heard the crunching sound of feet on stone chippings, but when he looked round, he was alone. He shivered, annoyed with himself for getting spooked by nothing. In a place like Highgate, with its blank-faced stone angels and moss-covered tombs, it was easy for one's imagination to run away with itself. But that shouldn't have been happening in this modern, functional garden of remembrance, with its wide, straight paths and neatly tended lawns.

Kees stood up, thinking about going back to the shopping center where he'd gotten off the bus and looking for somewhere to grab a cup of coffee. He had a little time to kill before he met up with Johnny, and the rain and his unhappy memories had sent a chill to his bones that he needed to dispel.

One of the neighboring graves caught his eye as he turned to leave. It was topped with a small stone statue that appeared to have been vandalized. At first, he thought he was looking at a ruined cherub, but on closer examination, he saw the figure was that of a prancing lion.

He took a startled pace backwards, unsure why the realization unsettled him so much. Perhaps it was the instinctive revulsion he experienced at the thought that someone would violate a grave, or perhaps because the image of a broken lion made his mind flash back to the night before. To the sight of Danny de Wit lying dead outside the Café de Tulpen, his golden hair spread out around him like a halo.

"Who would do something like this?"

"I've asked myself that a time or two, as well."

He hadn't realized he'd spoken aloud, or that he'd been overheard, until the reply came from behind him.

He turned to see a gray-haired man of around fifty, clutching a rake and dressed in plain navy overalls and heavy work boots. Was this the man whose footsteps Kees had heard earlier, on his way to tend one of the nearby flowerbeds?

"I'm sorry," Kees began. "I didn't mean..."

The gardener shook his head. "It's strange. Whoever's doing this seems to reserve their fury for that grave alone. Three times now in the last six months I've found that lion in pieces." His tone was resigned, as though nothing could really surprise him anymore.

Kees squinted at the writing beneath the statue, searching for a family name. He saw only the words 'Onze lieve zus'. Our dear sister.

Stop looking for some connection to Arjan. There isn't one. What did you think – that every time De Jager kills a member of the pride, he comes here and smashes that lion in some weird kind of ritual? Life doesn't work like that.

"Well, I hope you find the vandal soon," he said, brushing raindrops from the collar of his coat. "It must be awful to come here and find a mess like this."

The gardener nodded, then began to pick up shards of stone from around the damaged grave. Kees left him to the task.

As he reached the main entrance once more, his phone vibrated in his pocket. Out of respect for the sanctity of this place, he had set it to silent before walking through the gates.

The text message that had arrived came from Arjan.

Something's arisen at work. I need to go into the office and don't know how long I'll be there – may not be home till the small hours. Enjoy yourself with Johnny, and I'll see you tomorrow.

The guy was a workaholic, but then Kees had realized that pretty much as soon as he'd seen him in his office environment. He'd send a reply to Arjan once he was settled with a hot drink. After the shock of seeing the vandalized lion, he needed to be back amongst the bustle of everyday life more than ever.

First, he took a moment to call up the MP3 function on his phone. He jammed his headphones into his ears and scrolled down the playlist of his favorite albums till he found *Nevermind*.

Humming along to the music, he headed back to the Buikslotermeerplein at a brisk pace.

Chapter Ten

When Johnny had said he lived on the Brouwersgracht, Kees had pictured him owning a pricey apartment in one of the renovated warehouses that lined the pretty stretch of canal. Instead, he was surprised to found himself standing in front of a houseboat.

The floating homes of Amsterdam fell into two types. The first consisted of former working vessels, many of which had plied their trade along the IJ River, carrying freight to Belgium, Germany and beyond. The second were wooden, box-like constructions, purpose-built to provide living space. Johnny's home fell into the latter category.

Painted an arresting burgundy, it was one of the biggest houseboats on this side of the canal. A stretch of decking at the back of the boat was filled with an assortment of plants in terracotta pots, a couple of striped deckchairs, and, somewhat incongruously, a plastic flamingo that leaned at a drunken angle.

The flamingo wasn't the only thing that had captured Kees' attention. As he'd walked along the pavement, checking the house numbers, he'd spotted a small plaque fastened to one of the apartment blocks. Beneath a stylized image of a creature that had a lion's body and a man's head was what he assumed to be a date, 1752, and the words '*De Gulden Leeuw*'. The Golden Lion. The image couldn't help but remind him of his lover — part man, part beast.

'*We have been here as long as Amsterdam has been a city.*' Arjan's words echoed in his mind. Was this area an important part of the pride's territory, or was it another bizarre coincidence that this symbol should be so prominent on the street where Kees' best friend now lived? He thought back to the damaged gravestone, the ruined lion's face, and suppressed a shudder.

Kees crossed the short gangplank then knocked on the front door. If he'd had any doubts that this might be Johnny's home, the loud rock music he heard playing within erased them.

The door swung open. Johnny — barefoot and wearing only a pair of faded jeans — pulled Kees into an embrace.

"Great to see you, man. Come in." Johnny ushered Kees inside. "Sorry if the place is a bit of a mess. I was hoping to tidy up after I got out of the shower, but —"

"Yeah, I'm a bit early, I know." He had to raise his voice to be heard over the guitar riff blasting out from an iPod tethered to a small speaker dock. "I brought you these, by the way." He pressed a bag into Johnny's hand. It contained half a dozen bottles that he'd picked up in a specialist beer shop on his way over from the station.

"Thanks, I'll go put these in the fridge." Before he left the living room, Johnny turned the music down to a level that would make conversation easier.

Kees took the opportunity to explore the room. A gold disc hung on one wall, alongside a couple of photos. In one, Johnny and the rest of his band posed with the surviving members of Led Zeppelin. In the other, Kees and Johnny sat under some trees by a pond in the Vondelpark. That shot had been taken after the last of their exams, the summer they'd both turned eighteen. Within a few months, Kees had left Amsterdam for good. It brought a lump to his throat that even after everything Johnny had achieved, he chose to keep this photo of the two of them on display.

Johnny came back into the room, having pulled on a T-shirt and brushed his hair into some kind of order. He had a glass of beer in each hand. One he gave to Kees and the other he took a long drink from.

"That takes me back," Kees said, nodding to the photograph. "I was trying to remember the name of the girl who took the photo. You were going out with her, weren't you?"

"You mean Ans. Man, that was a long time ago, and I think we dated, like, three or four times."

It had been Johnny's pattern in those days. He'd flitted from girl to girl, seeing them for only a few weeks before getting bored and moving on to the next. Kees wondered quite how much his friend had changed in that respect, given that the last time they'd spoken, Johnny had mentioned something about being 'between wives' at the moment.

They went to sit on the low, comfortable couch, Johnny slouching casually with his arm thrown back against the top of the cushion. "So, what brings you to Amsterdam, Kees? You didn't say too much in your phone call."

"Well, it's all a bit hush-hush, but I'm investigating someone who appears to be sabotaging a computer project they're working on."

"Sounds exciting. Did you ever catch the guy who was selling the designs for those video games to a rival company?"

Kees had been trying to solve that particular problem the last time he and Johnny had met up. He nodded. "Yes, we got him in the end. He's doing eighteen months in prison for corporate theft... But what about you? You said something about getting ready to record a new album?"

Johnny nodded. "Yeah. We've been getting the material ready for a few months now." He waved a hand in the direction of his iPod. "Tyler sent me these guitar tracks he's been laying down and the tunes are strong, some of the best he's ever come up with. And we go into the studio in a few days. We've booked some time at Wisseloord, over in Hilversum. All the big names have recorded there—Golden Earring, The Scorpions, Def Leppard, Judas Priest... You'll have to come over, hang out with us."

"Sounds like fun, but I could have wrapped up what I'm doing here by then."

"So take some holiday. You work way too hard, Kees. When was the last time you just kicked back and had some fun?" Johnny turned an accusing look on him. "Or are you planning to up and leave without a proper goodbye, like you did last time?"

"I'm sorry, Johnny. I had my reasons for going. I just couldn't share them with anyone at the time."

"It had something to do with that party, didn't it? The one at the squatters' place."

Kees squirmed, not liking the serious turn the conversation had taken. "What makes you say that?"

"You were never quite the same after that night. I couldn't put my finger on it, but I knew you'd changed somehow."

He'd hoped there would never be a need to have this conversation, but Johnny needed answers, and only Kees could supply them. "Yeah, you're right. It was because of the party. There's something I never told you. I—I met someone there, and I lost my virginity to him."

"Kees van der Veer, you sly dog! You kept that quiet."

"Well, it turned out at the time that he was only looking for a one-night thing. But because he was my first, I kind of took it as a personal rejection—like I was too young and too inexperienced for him." The words tumbled out, with Kees not caring if Johnny thought that was a naïve reaction. "And I just wanted to get away from Amsterdam. This isn't the biggest city in the world, after all. There was always the chance I might bump into him, see him with someone else, and I couldn't bear that."

"You should have said something, Kees."

"I couldn't. I mean... I didn't even have the guts to tell you that I was into guys. I didn't know how you would react."

"What, you thought I might have stopped being your friend if I knew you were gay?"

"I know. I was crazy to think like that, but this guy... You want your first time to be something special, and it was. He shook my world up, you know?"

"Oh, we've all been there." The grin faded from Johnny's face. "And it feels great at the time, but it's not what you should base a relationship on. You need more in common than just great sex. Shame I had to find that out the hard way, with Franca."

Kees knew Johnny referred to his first wife. She'd clearly been the first girl to make any kind of lasting impression on the flighty Johnny, but they'd married and divorced by the time he was twenty-three. It had been a messy business, by all accounts, and Kees wished he'd been around to help his friend through that difficult period. But in those days, he'd been too wrapped up in his own hurt to pay attention to anyone else's.

"And what about Martine?" She had been Johnny's second wife. When Kees had last seen Johnny, at Madison Square Garden, the couple had just split up.

"Oh, she was having great sex, all right... She just wasn't having it with me..." Johnny swallowed the last of his beer and gestured to Kees' glass. "Can I get you another?"

Surprised to discover he'd finished his own drink, Kees nodded. He followed Johnny through into the houseboat's small, functional kitchen, and leaned against the doorframe while his friend took two fresh bottles of beer from the refrigerator.

"So, do you think you'll get married again?" he asked.

"If the right woman comes along. Being in a band, you're never short of offers, but I'm looking for someone who wants me for me, you know. Not just because I'm a fabulously wealthy, shit-hot bass player with an enormous dick..."

"Who also happens to be incredibly modest."

The two men cracked up laughing.

Kees hadn't realized till now just how much he'd missed spending time with Johnny. He had friends in the States, of course, but none with whom he had this same easy connection—this ability to pick up where they'd last left off, no matter how many years had intervened.

"But the good news is that the annulment was granted a couple of weeks ago. I am now officially a single man once more. Which is worth drinking to, wouldn't you say?" He raised his glass in a mock salute. "Anyway, you were telling me about that guy at the party. And don't say there's nothing more to tell, because I know you too well for that."

"You're right. There is more." Kees walked back into the living area, then took his seat on the couch once more. When Johnny joined him, he continued with his story, "And now we get to the weird part. When he left me that night, he told me we'd be together again, but he didn't give me his name, his number, or any way of ever getting hold of him. And like I said, I didn't want to see him again—not after the way he'd treated me. I thought— Well, I don't know what I thought. Maybe he was just softening the blow of rejecting me."

Johnny nodded, as if he knew all the ways of letting a lover down gently.

"But he spoke with this absolute certainty, Johnny. As if our being together was written in the stars. Then, a few days ago, I turn up at the offices of the company who've got me looking for this saboteur, and there he is. Sitting behind a desk, large as life, looking at me like we've never been apart…"

"And why do I get the feeling you're doing more than just working for him?"

Kees blushed under the strength of his friend's direct look. "Okay, you've got me there. Yes, I'm sleeping with him, and it's just as good as it was all those years ago. Johnny, I've never met anyone like

Arjan. He's intelligent, he's charming, he's unbelievably hot." *And he can shift into the shape of a lion at will.* He decided to keep that last piece of information to himself.

"You've got it bad, haven't you? I recognize all the signs."

"I'm crazy about him. And it scares me. Not because of what you said about sex not being enough, because I know there's more to our relationship than that. But I'm only going to be here for a few weeks at best. What happens when I have to go back to New York?"

"Kees, if you want something badly enough, you'll find a way to make it happen. I always have."

"Have you thought you might not be the best role model in this particular situation? I mean, you are speaking as a man with two" — he held up two fingers, to emphasize the point — "divorces behind him."

"Hey, I never went into either of those marriages thinking they wouldn't last. And with experience comes wisdom, as someone with a lot more of both those qualities than me once said." Johnny's face brightened, as if a light bulb had just been switched on, and he reached for a notepad and pen that lay on the low coffee table. "Now that's a line I have to use…"

Johnny scribbled a few words on the topmost sheet of paper. Kees realized those must be the lyrics for the band's new album. He tried to read them upside down, but could make no sense of his friend's sprawling handwriting.

"Man, you and I should spend more time together. We always were a hell of a team. I've missed having you to bounce off, you know?" Johnny seemed about to add something else, then his phone started vibrating, moving a little way across the table as it did.

He reached for it, clearly about to dismiss the call, then appeared to register the name on the caller display. "Sorry, I'm going to have to take this. It's Tyler. You don't mind?"

"Not at all."

Kees half-listened as Johnny spoke to his bandmate.

"They said yes? At such short notice?" Johnny slapped the couch cushion beside him, a triumphant look on his face. "See, what am I always telling you about fate? Yeah, I know... Okay, I'll speak to you later. I've got Kees with me and we're catching up on old times... I will. Bye, Tyler."

"Good news?" Kees asked when Johnny had set the phone back on the table.

"Yeah, we've been looking for somewhere to play a low-key gig, try out a couple of the new songs. Well, Tyler's managed to get us a slot at Hemel en Aarde next Friday."

Kees shot Johnny a quizzical look. "Hemel en Aarde?"

"Oh, that's right. Of course you wouldn't know where that is. The fun I'm going to have, filling in the gaps in your local knowledge..." He sipped at his beer before continuing. "The place opened about four years ago, in one of the old municipal buildings on the Rokin. It's mostly a dance club, but they put on gigs, too. Only holds a couple of hundred people, so it's perfect for what we have in mind. Come along, Kees. I'll put you on the guest list. And you can bring this mystery man of yours."

Kees was about to demur, not sure that a rock concert would be Arjan's scene. Then he reconsidered. Why shouldn't he show his lover something of his own world, introduce him to his oldest and dearest friend? "Thanks, Johnny, I'd like that."

"Then it's settled. Once I know what time the doors will be opening, I'll text you the details. And I'm looking forward to meeting the guy who's been your secret obsession all these years."

"By the way," Kees said, keen to steer the conversation away from Arjan, "there's something I wanted to ask you. Do you know anything about that plaque on the building across the way? Something to do with *De Gulden Leeuw*?"

"Yeah. It commemorates the old brewery that used to stand where those apartment blocks are now. I did some research into the area when I was first thinking of buying a houseboat, and it turns out there used to be several breweries round here. The Golden Lion was the oldest established, I think."

Kees nodded. It made sense. Brouwersgracht meant 'Brewer's canal', after all. But he still couldn't help thinking of Arjan, and whether the de Wits might have any connection to the brewing trade. They seemed to have a link to every other major industry in the city, after all.

"Do you have plans for dinner?" Johnny asked. "If not, I'll ring one of the Chinese restaurants over on Zeedijk, get some take-out for both of us."

At the mention of Chinese food, Kees found his mouth watering. "That sounds like a great idea. Though I warn you, I haven't got any better at eating with chopsticks since we last had dim sum."

"That's settled, then. I'll just go dig out a menu..."

Johnny strolled into the kitchen. Kees rested his head against the back of the couch and nursed his beer glass, filled with a profound sense of wellbeing. At this moment, everything seemed right in the world. He was back in the city he loved, spending time with his best friend. For all Arjan feared he might somehow be in danger, having made himself visible to De Jager, he felt safe and wanted here. He closed his eyes, and wondered whether he should go for char siu pork with noodles or chicken with ginger and spring onions.

Chapter Eleven

A blast of warm air hit Arjan as he walked through the sliding doors and into the bustling lobby. Normally, he wouldn't have chosen to arrange a meeting in such bland surroundings as an airport hotel, but today the location suited his needs. He'd hated having to lie about where he was going, but the less Kees knew about the real reason for this rendezvous, the better.

The man he'd come here to see sat in a low-backed leather armchair in the lounge, sipping from a small white cup. If Arjan knew his father, he'd be drinking the strongest coffee the hotel could provide, black, sweetened with a generous spoonful of sugar.

Cornelis de Wit rose from his chair as Arjan approached. Even though his hair was now more white than gold and there were deep wrinkles etched at the corners of his eyes, he was still an exceptionally handsome man. Arjan couldn't help but notice a couple of women sitting at a nearby table discreetly checking his father out. How, he wondered, would they react if they knew the man was in his late eighties, and his striking looks were due to him being of genetic stock that was not human?

One of the women, a plump, middle-aged redhead, glanced at Arjan as he strode past. He flashed a little smile at her and noticed a flush appear on her pale cheeks. Even though he had no interest in her, it would have been rude not to at least acknowledge her open appreciation of him.

He greeted his father in the traditional Dutch fashion, embracing him and pressing three swift kisses on alternating cheeks.

Cornelis did not look pleased to see him. "Arjan, why the hell did you drag me all the way out here? On a Saturday evening, too."

"It's nice to see you as well, Papa." Arjan settled into the armchair opposite Cornelis', and caught the attention of a passing waiter. "Could I get a sparkling water, please?" He glanced over at his father. "And anything for you?"

Cornelis shook his head.

Once the man had gone to fetch his drink, Arjan said, "I know you'd rather be at home with Mama, tending to your rose bushes, but I didn't want to run the risk of being seen at your place. You never know who might be watching us."

"Isn't this all rather overdramatic?" Cornelis grumped.

"Not at all. You know what I need to talk to you about."

"Yes, yes. De Jager." Cornelis sounded weary, as if he'd discussed this matter far too many times before.

As far as Arjan was concerned, they couldn't speak about it enough. Much as he loved his father, the old man had become complacent. That, he supposed, came of growing up in a time when the threat from their oldest enemy had all but faded into the distance. Cornelis de Wit had watched his own father play his part in the Second World War, stalking the occupying army from the shadows, and had lived all his adult life in a city that had become one of the most tolerant and welcoming of diversity. Arjan was sure it must be hard for Cornelis to contemplate that the hard-won freedom of the pride to live free from persecution was now under threat. But that threat was all too real. The deaths of Anneke, Wim and now Danny, killed in such a shocking, public fashion, were all the proof Arjan needed.

"Papa, this is not some figment of my imagination. I was there when he murdered Danny."

"And you're really sure that was De Jager? I read the papers all the time, you know. So many terrible things happen every day. All the drugs and the gang-related crime..."

Now Cornelis sounded every year of his age, an old man seeking to hide himself away from the perceived dangers of modern life.

"How many more of us have to die before you start taking this seriously?" He kept his voice low, not wanting to attract attention.

The waiter arrived with his drink, and the bill. Arjan paid him before fixing his father with a steady look. "We need to be taking steps to protect ourselves. Everyone needs to be aware that De Jager is a very real and present threat. After Uncle Danny, who's next? Mama? You?"

"This is a matter that should be raised in a full pride meeting, not here." Cornelis seemed determined to give no ground.

"I'm fully aware of that, but you know my authority within the pride is tenuous at best, even as your son.

But if you talk, people listen. And right now, I really need them to listen. Please, Papa, you know what you have to do."

For a long moment, it seemed that his father would dismiss the request out of hand. Then Cornelis set down his empty cup and gave a curt nod.

"Very well. I'll convene the others, and let you know when I've arranged it. Though I still think you have all this out of proportion. Why, after all this time, would the families resume hostilities with us? Have they forgotten how we fought alongside them when they were most in need of allies?"

"Who knows?" The question had nagged at Arjan for some time. "But the world is changing, and not necessarily for the better. People will always find reason to be afraid of those who are different and if they feel they're under threat, then they'll lash out."

"We are no threat to them. Never have been. We just want to exist alongside them in harmony. Why can't they see that?"

"Maybe they don't want to. But I'm not going to just sit back and let De Jager keep picking us off. If he wants a fight, I'm quite prepared to give him one."

Cornelis sighed. "All I ask is that you don't do anything rash, at least not until I've spoken with the rest of the pride. It may be that after the meeting, you're on your own."

He stood, and Arjan couldn't help but notice that his father's movements were not quite as fluid as they had once been. Even though Cornelis retained an aura of quietly controlled strength, his time as the pride leader was almost over. Once, Arjan would have been considered the natural successor. Now, from his position on the fringes, he would only be able to watch the other candidates fight it out between themselves.

"I'd love to stay and chat with you," Cornelis said, "but it's getting late, and your mother and I have arranged to go and see Lise at her apartment. See how she's holding up."

"Of course, I understand."

"That doesn't mean we don't want you to come over soon. Betje was only saying the other day she can't remember the last time she made a meal for you."

Arjan's stomach rumbled at the thought of his mother's hearty home cooking. It would be nice to go to their big home in the south of the city for dinner, even nicer if Kees were by his side.

"I'd love to. And I'd like to bring a guest."

For the first time since their conversation had begun, Cornelis fixed his son with a warm smile, recognizing something in the tone of Arjan's request. "So, you've met someone new, have you?"

"Yes. And…he's the one."

Cornelis raised an eyebrow. "You sound very sure of that."

"I know he is. I've known for a long time. It's just never been possible for us to be together, until now."

"I'm intrigued. And I'm sure Betje will be delighted to meet this special person." Cornelis clapped Arjan on the back. "We'll speak soon. Take care of yourself."

"You, too, Papa."

Well, that went better than I'd hoped. Arjan watched his father stride out in the direction of the lobby. He still wasn't confident that the old man would make a concerted attempt to warn the rest of the pride about the danger they were in, but at least they seemed to have reached some kind of accord.

A quick glance at his watch confirmed that he still had time to kill before night fell. He considered walking over to the main airport building and browsing in the mall, then dismissed the idea. Shopping for shopping's sake had never been his idea of fun.

Instead, he picked up the menu that lay on the table and ordered a roast beef sandwich and a glass of cabernet sauvignon. He'd need to keep his energy levels up for later, after all.

As he ate, savoring the taste of the rare meat, Arjan wondered what Kees might be doing right now. Really, he knew so little about his lover, even though the man had been a constant part of his thoughts for so many years. But learning about what made him tick — his favorite foods, his taste in music, the things he liked to do in bed — was such a delightful process.

Thinking of the last time he and Kees had fucked sent a rush of heat to Arjan's groin, and he felt his cock begin to stir. This was definitely not the time or place to get an erection, but it took some considerable effort on his part to will it away.

* * * *

In control of himself once more, he left the hotel and went to find a taxi. His other reason for arranging to meet his father here was the airport's proximity to the forest that dominated the fringes of the city's southern suburbs, the Amsterdamse Bos.

The Bos was unique in that it was completely man-made. A project that had begun in the 1930s, the planting and landscaping had taken over thirty years to complete and had provided work for the city's residents at a time of high unemployment. It had been designed as a place of relaxation, where people could enjoy activities such as cycling, horse riding, fishing and swimming. Anyone who was not aware of the forest's history would find it hard to believe the winding streams and meadows dotted with little groves of trees had not been here for centuries.

For Arjan and the rest of his urbanized pride, the Bos was the closest they could achieve to experiencing a wild, natural environment. Since Danny's death, he had been driven by the need to run free, to rid himself of the tension that had built within him. He'd already scared Kees half to death by shifting in front of him, and he had no desire to do that again.

The taxi driver didn't question why Arjan wanted to be dropped off at the forest's main entrance after sundown. Alongside its many other leisure facilities, the Bos had an extensive campsite. In his jeans and hooded fleece, and with a rucksack slung over his arm, Arjan looked just like any other visitor preparing to spend a night under canvas.

Cutting across a stretch of neatly maintained grass, he walked toward a large thicket of trees that would provide more than enough cover for his needs. Not that he was worried about being seen—the only populated areas of the forest at this time of night would be the camping area and the waterside restaurants on the shore of the Nieuwe Meer lake, and he had no intention to go anywhere near either of those places.

Quickly, Arjan stripped off his clothes, took off his watch and signet ring then stuffed all his belongings into the backpack, which he stashed under a bush. He took a deep breath, centering himself, then closed his eyes and let his body shift.

Chapter Twelve

Arjan wrinkled his nose, breathing in the scents that were borne on the night air. The Amsterdamse Bos was home to a number of species of farm animals, and he could distinctly make out the ripe stink of goats and the earthier scent of Scottish Highland cattle. His mouth watered at the thought of fresh meat, but even if the beasts had been living wild and not secured in their pens, his instinct would not have been to go after any of them. The pride's females were the natural hunters, like the big cats to whom they were related.

No, tonight was all about feeling the wind in his mane and the soft grass beneath his paws. He padded out of the thicket, slowly beginning to pick up the pace until he was covering the ground in a rapid lope. The beast within him had taken over, and Arjan lost himself in the thrill of running – of existing only for the moment. He retained enough caution to stay close to the treeline, just in case some late-night cyclist might come pedaling along the path toward him.

So what if someone sees me? Who'd believe their story if they said they were cycling through the Amsterdamse Bos when they saw a lion? It'll be written off as some drug-fueled hallucination. Too much time in the coffee shops and not enough out in the fresh air...

Allowing his jumbled thoughts to drift away to nothing, Arjan ran on through the dark woods. Somewhere in the branches high above his head, a night bird cried out in warning, and far in the distance, he could make out the sound of traffic rumbling by on the road to Schiphol.

With each stride he took, the pain and loss of his uncle's death receded further. Nothing could touch him here, nothing could hurt him anymore. He was cunning, powerful, invincible.

At last, he found himself back where he'd started, his circuit of the forest complete, his body close to exhaustion. It would be nice to curl up in a bed of leaves and fall asleep in his lion form, but he couldn't run the risk of being found in the morning, human in appearance and all too naked.

Instead, he shifted back and pulled on his clothes. Once he was dressed, he headed for the park entrance. It was already gone midnight, and the thought of waiting in the cold for the last bus back to the center of Amsterdam didn't appeal — assuming he hadn't missed it already. He called up the number of the taxi firm that had brought him to the park and ordered a cab.

In less than ten minutes, he was on his way home, dozing as the miles passed and half-aware of the soft rock station on the car radio. He'd asked the driver to drop him off on the Prinsengracht, but as they neared the apartment, an impulse struck him, too powerful to ignore.

Leaning forward in his seat, Arjan asked the driver, "Would you mind taking me to Herenstraat?"

"Of course. Whatever you want."

The driver dropped him off on the corner of Herenstraat. Standing on the pavement, he gazed up at the apothecary's sign that adorned the building where Kees was staying and wondered whether he'd made a mistake. For all he knew, Kees was out with Johnny, clubbing or even just catching up on old times over drinks. Most of the city center bars stayed open till at least two in the morning on Saturdays, and in a few places, it was possible to stay quite comfortably till the sun came up.

If he isn't in I'll go to the brown café round the corner, and treat myself to a nightcap, then I'll go home. He pressed the buzzer, and waited. Just at the point when he had given up on Kees answering, a sleepy voice said, "Hello?"

"Kees, it's Arjan. I didn't mean to wake you up. I'm sorry, I'll go."

"No, no, it's fine," came the reply. "I'll come down and let you in."

He should have brought wine or a box of the nutty *kletskoppen* cookies that Kees liked. Anything to soften the blow of rousing his lover from sleep.

When Kees answered the door, Arjan saw that he wore only a pair of striped boxer shorts that had been pulled on back to front in the man's haste to make himself look decent. His hair was mussed up, and he rubbed at his eyes. Arjan thought he'd never seen him looking quite so vulnerable — or so appealing. He could have jumped on Kees right there in the doorway, but he quickly squashed down the impulse.

"This was really not a good idea," he muttered, half to himself. "Maybe I should leave you till tomorrow."

"No, please, don't go," Kees begged him. "Come to bed."

They climbed the narrow stairs to Kees' apartment. Even before they were through the front door, Kees mashed his lips to Arjan's in an urgent kiss.

"Hey, what's got into you?" Arjan asked, as Kees pushed his hands up under the hem of the fleece, seeking to burrow beneath his T-shirt, too.

"Just horny," Kees admitted, sounding considerably more awake, "and I want you."

He'd never been quite so forward in all the time they'd been together, usually letting Arjan take the lead. Arjan couldn't help wondering what had brought about this change in attitude.

"Have you been smoking something tonight? Popping any pills?"

Kees shook his head in vehement denial. "I don't touch any of that stuff. Even Johnny doesn't have anything to do with drugs anymore, not since a guy in this band they toured with overdosed. Said it made him think twice about where he got his thrills…"

He broke off to press another sloppy kiss on Arjan. Their bodies ground together, and Arjan felt the solid bulk of Kees' cock hard up against his own.

"We had a few beers, though," Kees resumed his story. "And some good Chinese food. And we talked about life. I told Johnny about how much better mine's got since you came back into it." He grinned as he grabbed Arjan by the hand, dragging him into the bedroom.

"I'm glad to hear it."

"And I didn't give him any of the details, but I told him the sex we have is amazing. *A-maz-ing*," Kees repeated for emphasis. "But I don't want to talk about it. I want to do it. So come on, Arjan. Get naked for me. Show me that big, hard cock of yours."

This demanding, dirty-talking side of Kees was something new, but Arjan couldn't deny that he liked it. For the second time that night, he peeled out of his clothes, though this time he didn't think about stowing them neatly away, simply let them lay where they fell on Kees' bedroom floor.

As they fell on the bed together, Kees reached out and trailed a finger over Arjan's back. "This scratch is fresh," he commented. "Does it hurt?"

Arjan twisted his head, but couldn't see the injury Kees had noticed. He turned so that he could see himself in the mirrored wardrobe door. He vaguely remembered scraping against a thorn bush as he'd been running through the forest, but until it had been pointed out, he hadn't even been aware he'd torn his skin. The pure adrenaline that came from letting his inner lion take over had dulled his senses to the pain.

"You know," he said, "I didn't even realize I'd done that."

"There's something different about you tonight." Kees continued to caress Arjan's skin, moving lower until he was tracing a digit over the furrow between Arjan's buttocks. "And I'm not sure what it is. All I know is that you smell of sweat and man, and I like it."

"Good. I must remember that you like to be surprised, and you like me not to shower." He took hold of Kees' hand, stilling him in his progress. "Now roll over and let me fuck you."

Kees shook his head, all his sleepiness vanished. In its place was a kind of authority Arjan had never noticed in him before. "Not tonight. We're going to do things my way."

Arjan raised an eyebrow in surprise. "Really? And what way might that be?"

"I bought something the other day. Something I thought you'd like. But I really have to be in charge here. And to make sure that happens, I have to do this…"

As he spoke, he grabbed Arjan's left wrist. Before Arjan could respond, he felt something being wrapped around it. When he heard the rasp of Velcro strips being pressed together, he realized he'd been fastened into a cuff. Even as he struggled to try to free himself, Kees worked to tether his left wrist, too. In moments, he found himself securely bound to the bedframe, and though the beast in him raged at the indignity, his dick surged up, revealing just how much the rest of him liked the sensation.

"Kees, what are you doing? Let me go or so help me…" In truth, his protests were only for show. The switch from his usual dominant role was proving too intriguing to resist.

"Nuh-huh. I call the shots now and you can't deny you want this." Kees sounded defiant, as though part of him couldn't quite believe he had his strong, self-assured lover tied to the bed.

"Yes, yes, I want this," Arjan admitted. "Whatever this actually is."

"Oh, you'll find out." Kees took a moment to root in the drawer of his nightstand. When he brought out the object he'd been searching for, Arjan gaped at him in disbelief. It was a small, bullet-style vibrator.

"You can't be serious," Arjan said, even as a thrill of dark pleasure shot through him.

"Don't worry. If you want me to stop, you just have to say so." Kees grinned. "Though trust me… I don't think that will happen."

When he switched on the toy, a low, steady buzzing filled the air. The smile never fading from his face,

Kees played the little vibrator over the insides of Arjan's thighs.

"Kees, please..." His muscles seemed to be tensing of their own volition, reacting to the unexpected stimulation.

"Please what? Stop? Go on? Because from the way your cock's reacting, I'd say you're enjoying this."

When he looked down the length of his own body, Arjan saw how full and proud his erection had grown. He lay there, helpless to do anything as Kees moved the bullet higher, until it was dangerously close to the entrance of his arse. Just the thought that his lover might decide to slip it inside that tight passage had him writhing against the sheets. Though he usually liked to be the one who did the penetrating, he was as receptive as any other man when it came to having his arsehole played with.

"You want this, don't you?" Even as Kees spoke, he was teasing Arjan's opening with the very tip of the vibrator.

Arjan growled out his answer, "Yes, I want it. Don't make me beg, Kees."

"Would I really be so cruel?" Kees smirked, his expression making any answer redundant. He pulled the toy away from Arjan's body just long enough to give it a liberal coating of lube, then he pressed it back where it had been. This time, it breached the muscular ring and popped inside. Even though less than an inch of the thing was inside his hole, it still managed to send its vibrations right to Arjan's core.

"Oh, fuck..." The curse slipped from his lips, and he blushed at the strength of his reaction. He wasn't accustomed to ceding control, and he knew Kees must be loving every moment of this.

Kees kept tight hold of the vibrator. He seemed to know just how long he could keep it buried in Arjan's arse before the pleasure threatened to become too much and Arjan spilled his seed.

As Kees pulled it free, Arjan clawed at the sheets, almost beyond rational thought. The next thing he knew, Kees had donned a condom and was climbing on top of him. He'd expected to be freed from the cuffs before they fucked, but Kees appeared to be working to an agenda of his own devising.

With his hands still restrained, Arjan couldn't move to wrap his arms around Kees, or even touch his own fiercely aching cock. He just had to lie there as Kees slid his cock home. His arsehole still quivered with aftershocks, little reminders of the vibrator's insistent presence.

"You see... This is how you tame the beast..." Kees whispered against Arjan's ear as he began to thrust.

"You'll never tame me," Arjan retorted defiantly. "Try all you want, Kees, but when I'm free of these cuffs, I'll show you who's really on top around here."

"Promises, promises." Kees increased the speed of his strokes, powering hard into Arjan's supine, willing body.

Arjan thrashed, trying to achieve enough in the way of movement to free himself from his bonds, but his efforts were in vain. His fingers curled convulsively, and he looked into Kees' soft brown eyes, swept away by the pleasure that started somewhere at the root of his cock and spread out in sharp bursts throughout his body.

He and Kees came in almost the same instant, Arjan's cum arching up to land in pearly strings across his abs.

Once Kees had withdrawn from inside him, Arjan flapped his hand in a wordless gesture. Kees moved to release the bindings, and placed a gentle kiss on the inside of each of Arjan's wrists.

Such a beautiful way for the night to end, he thought, as he gathered Kees to him. Maybe in time he'd tell him about his adventures in the Amsterdamse Bos tonight, and the thrill of running free with the wind blowing through his mane. But not right now, not when it felt so good to lie here and think about nothing but this perfect moment spent in his lover's arms.

Chapter Thirteen

Kees strolled back into the office that was the base for the Excelsior employees working on the cryptocurrency project. Already he was on his third mug of coffee of the day, and still the figures scrolling up the computer screens showed nothing out of the ordinary.

He was the only person in the building. Even Luuk, the company's security guard, had been given the day off, and there was something a little unsettling about being alone here, with nothing but the steady hum of the air conditioning system to break the silence.

From the break room, where the tea and coffee-making facilities were kept, he'd been able to hear the sound of merrymakers on the street outside. The King's Day celebrations were in full swing. Bunting and strings of balloons hung from the balconies of almost every building he'd passed on the way here, and people strolled by, their faces painted with the red, white and blue of the Dutch flag. It seemed like everyone was dressed from head to foot in orange, whether that be T-shirts and tracksuit bottoms, pretty prom dresses or replica football shirts. Kees had even seen one man walking along in an orange ballgown, accessorized with elbow-length opera gloves and a necklace made from carrots. A Chihuahua wearing an orange tutu, a tiny tiara perched on its head, had trotted alongside him on a lead.

Later, there would be bands playing and DJs setting up in the big public squares, but Kees doubted his work would be finished in time for him to catch any of the festivities. He'd satisfied himself that Thijs Kempen wasn't responsible for leaking information, but that still left the computers of both Eline Vos and Rob van Bergen to check for any signs of suspicious activity. From time to time, he watched one of the TV crime shows that featured the work of forensic experts, and the ease with which they managed to crack a case often had him yelling at the screen with frustration. Nothing was ever that simple in his experience. But, he supposed, if viewers were treated to the reality of the job—with storylines where someone took several days to crack a password— ratings for those programs would soon plummet.

He wished he could ring Arjan and talk to him about how his investigations were progressing. Maybe the conversation would take an intimate turn, and they'd find themselves engaging in phone sex, describing all the delightfully rude things they wanted to do to each other. But Arjan had a long-standing invitation to a barbecue in Amstelveen, at the home of Excelsior's finance director, and Kees couldn't see him wanting to talk dirty in that kind of environment.

Glancing back at the screens, Kees noticed something that made him sit up a little straighter in his chair. Results were beginning to pop up on Rob's machine. Just scraps of data here and there, but enough to indicate that, like Thijs, the man had been deleting emails.

As Kees looked more closely, words began to stand out, making the hairs on the back of his neck prickle. This wasn't a case of someone getting rid of private messages to a girlfriend. If what he read was to be believed, the arrangements that had been made here were of a much more sinister nature. Though he didn't recognize the names of all the substances involved, he knew enough to realize that Rob van Bergen was dealing drugs.

Obviously, Rob believed he'd done enough to cover his tracks. This was the second pass of the file recovery software on his machine, and it was becoming clear that he'd deleted the incriminating messages using a program that wrote new data over old, making them much harder to retrieve. Kees also suspected that most of the transactions had been carried out over the Deep Web, the part of the Internet not immediately accessible to standard search engines. Only those who knew the correct terms to type in would be able to retrieve the information they craved. Not all the sites on the Deep Web were hubs for illegal activity, but if someone was looking for access to extreme pornography, hard drugs and unlicensed firearms, they would be sure to find it.

Proving his suspicions would involve the use of a dedicated web crawler, in addition to running a program designed to root out deliberately hidden data and IP addresses. It would take a while and, strictly speaking, it didn't fall within the scope of his original investigation. But he couldn't ignore what he'd discovered and he was certain Arjan wouldn't want him to.

It wasn't much of a stretch to assume that if Rob were prepared to sell drugs, then he would also be happy to sell the details of Excelsior's cryptocurrency software. As time passed, though, Kees failed to see anything in the fragments of email conversation to support his theory.

By a process of elimination, that had to mean Eline was the mole. The software running on her laptop had failed to turn up anything yet, but Kees was prepared to keep on searching for as long as it took. As Arjan had pointed out, he had a very high success rate, and he hadn't achieved that by giving up at the first attempt before.

Knowing he shouldn't really interrupt Arjan when he was socializing with his colleagues, he reached for his phone anyway. When Arjan answered, Kees could hear music playing, and children's voices squealing and chattering.

"Hey, Kees."

"Arjan, sounds like someone's having a good time there."

"Yeah. Gerard hired a bouncy castle for all the neighborhood kids. Give it a couple of hours and a few more glasses of sangria and the adults'll be on that thing, too."

"Well, I apologize for ringing, but I have news for you that can't wait. I don't have the evidence to prove it just yet, but I'm convinced that Eline is the saboteur. That's not why I'm calling, though."

"Go on." Arjan's interest had clearly been piqued.

"You're really not going to like this, but I'm turning up emails that suggest Rob van Bergen is a drug dealer. Some of what he's selling is legal highs, I think, but there are also references to speed and cocaine. Not only does he have clients across the city, he looks to be shipping the stuff out to buyers in Germany and the UK. And I wondered what you want to do about it."

"Do just as you would for any other case. Give me all the information you can collate, and I'll deal with Rob as I see appropriate." Arjan gave a deep sigh. "It'll be a shame to lose him, but if what you're saying is true, then dismissal is my only option. And if I have to get rid of Eline, too…"

"I'm sure you'll be able to find decent replacements for them, given your reputation within the industry," Kees reassured him.

"A reputation that'll be in shreds as soon as it gets out that my employees are carrying out illegal acts on company time."

"Don't look at it like that, Arjan. What Rob's been up to could happen in any industry."

"I know. It just seems like the bad news will never stop coming… Oh, I have to go, Kees. The steaks are ready."

"Last time I went to a barbecue, the burgers they served were still raw in the middle," Kees recalled with a shudder. "Though I don't suppose that would be too much of a problem for you."

"Less of your cheek, or there'll be trouble," Arjan warned, but he was laughing as he ended the call.

Kees turned back to the computer screen, and continued his search for the material that would prove Eline Vos' guilt beyond doubt.

* * * *

It took him the rest of the day and into the early hours of the morning, but at last he began to piece together a trail that led from Eline to a man she referred to only as Wolf. First the Hunter, now this…

Kees was beginning to wonder when Little Red Riding Hood would make an appearance.

He would need to check dates and times with the information that he could acquire from her colleagues' computers, but it seemed that every time a significant step forward was taken in the design of the software, Eline had informed Wolf of it. She'd been passing changes to the code onto him almost as fast as they could be produced.

What he still didn't understand was her reason for sabotaging her own work. As far as he could see, no money was changing hands and no threat of blackmail hung over Eline's head, no indication that Wolf had information about her she wouldn't want making public. Maybe she was doing this simply because she got some kind of thrill from it.

Kees looked through the notes he'd made one more time. Eline looked to have been given Wolf's details by someone called Simon. From reading the snippets of conversation he'd recovered, it wasn't hard to work out this was her boyfriend, the guy with the ratty dreadlocks who'd come to collect her outside the office. Kees still couldn't discount the possibility that Simon had been pressuring Eline into giving up the code, even if she wasn't doing so to bail him out financially. If that were the case, however, he couldn't work out the connection between Simon and Wolf, nor whether Wolf acted alone or was the front for a larger group. He needed to think like a hacker in order to discover the motivations of all the parties involved, but despite the help of a steady intake of caffeine, his eyelids were drooping and he found it increasingly difficult to stay awake.

Dawn was breaking as, finally, he copied all the files and oddments of data he'd retrieved onto a flash drive, so they could be passed to Arjan. He had to make sure to leave no trace of his presence on the computers he'd been examining. Only when he was satisfied that no one would realize he'd ever been in this room did he leave the deserted building, and walk out to a street where bunting still fluttered and the litter left behind by King's Day revelers waited to be cleared away.

Chapter Fourteen

"Ah, Rob, do come in."

Arjan waited for Rob van Bergen to take the one free seat before his desk. Kees already sat in the other chair.

The young man ran a hand through his light brown hair, already thinning — even though he was barely into his twenties — and looked around. He seemed distracted and anxious, a reaction Arjan would probably have put down to his being pulled away from his work if he hadn't been informed of Rob's extra-curricular activities. *Does he know he's been found out? And if so, is he already concocting his excuses?*

"Rob, I'd like you to meet Kees van der Veer. Kees works in the field of corporate espionage."

Kees gave a small nod of acknowledgment. Rob said nothing.

"I brought Kees into the company when it became obvious that someone was deliberately leaking information about the cryptocurrency project."

"And what does that have to do with me?" Rob's voice was tight. "Because if you're suggesting that I would be involved in something like that, you're wrong."

"Don't worry, Rob. We know you're blameless where that's concerned. But in the course of his very thorough investigations, Kees discovered your little sideline."

"I don't know what you're talking about," Rob said defiantly.

So he was going to try to bluff this out. "Don't play the innocent." Arjan brandished the flash drive Kees had given him. A copy of the information it contained was already securely backed up and in the safe in his apartment. "Everything is on here – dates, quantities, addresses of the people you've been selling to..."

"Oh, come on. You can't be serious. I'm not giving people anything they can't get in the head shops on the Nieuwe Hoogstraat."

"I wish it were true, Rob, but we all know that it's not. Legal highs are one thing, and if that really was the only thing involved, we might have been able to find some way of keeping you with the company. You're one of the best software engineers we have, and that's what makes all of this so hard to understand. You're well rewarded, well respected... Why the hell would you want to throw all this away by selling hard drugs?"

Rob just shook his head from side to side, a bewildered expression on his face, as if he really didn't have a logical explanation. Perhaps he'd thought there were fewer risks involved in dealing online, rather than face-to-face. Maybe he'd never believed he would get caught. But for whatever reason, when temptation had come calling, he hadn't been able to resist.

Arjan picked up the phone and dialed reception. "Karin, could you send Luuk through to my office, please? Thank you." He looked at Rob. "Luuk's going to take you back to your office. You'll have five minutes to clear your desk, then you'll be escorted from the premises. In the meantime, I'll be asking everyone in the company to change their passwords, in case you get any bright ideas about trying to access our servers or email system remotely. And just think yourself lucky that I'm not going to get the police involved here."

The big security guard entered the room. Rob rose and went with him. Once he'd gone, Arjan rubbed his face with both hands, then addressed Kees, "I keep wondering if I should have been harder on him."

"You did what you had to," Kees replied simply.

"And that was the easy part." Arjan sighed. "What comes next is much harder." He punched another extension number into the phone. "Eline, this is Arjan. I'd like to see you in my office, right away."

Eline arrived within moments. Whether she'd seen Rob packing up his belongings Arjan didn't know, but she seemed calm and even managed a smile as she walked in.

"You wanted to see me, *meneer*?"

"Yes, please take a seat." He paused, wondering where to begin, and sure the strain must be etched on his face. "You'll have to excuse me, but I'm having a rather difficult day. First of all, I've had to let one of your colleagues go because it turns out he's been dealing drugs on company time…"

"So that's why Rob was—" Her eyes widened, the news obviously coming as a genuine surprise to her. "I thought it might have something to do with all that hacking business."

"Ah, yes, 'that hacking business', as you so charmingly put it. You sound remarkably blasé about the situation, given how much extra work it's been causing you over the last few months. But then, you've been more prepared for that than either Thijs or Rob, haven't you?"

"I'm sure I have no idea what you mean."

Just like Rob, Eline seemed prepared to deny all knowledge of what she'd done.

"Please don't make this harder for either of us than it has to be, Eline. My friend Kees here" — and for the first time he made a point of gesturing to Kees — "was hired specifically to trace the source of all the leaks coming from your department. We have all the evidence that tells us you've been passing on code relating to the cryptocurrency project. What we don't understand is why."

He was giving her a chance to unburden herself, but Eline remained silent, picking at lint on her sweater.

"Is it Simon? Is he forcing you to pass the information on to somebody?" Arjan looked for some change in her expression, some indication that he was thinking along the right track.

She just shrugged. "I don't have to say anything to you."

"Then you can offer your excuses to the police. I think we're done here."

For the second time in less than ten minutes, Arjan was forced to inform a member of his staff that they were being let go, only this time there would be a criminal investigation into Eline's actions.

When Luuk had taken Eline to collect her possessions, Arjan stood up and stretched out his arms. A dull headache nagged behind his brow.

"So that's it, then," Kees said. His tone seemed strangely downbeat, not at all what Arjan would have suspected given the successful resolution of his work. "It's over."

"What do you mean?"

"Well, you've got all the information you need to begin a prosecution. Eline's probably going to be looking at a prison sentence, and you don't need my help anymore. I can start looking at arranging my flight back to New York."

"When...?" Arjan broke off. It hadn't occurred to him that Kees might already be thinking about leaving.

"Not for a few days. I want to stick around for Johnny's gig at Hemel en Aarde on Friday, at the very least."

Arjan sighed. "Do you think so little of me that you'd run straight back to the States at the first opportunity, just like you ran from me all those years ago?"

"Of course not. If it were possible, I'd stay here with you for as long as you want me. But I have a job to go back to. And if you really believe that I'm in danger from De Jager, doesn't it make more sense for me to get as far away from him as I can?"

His words made perfect sense. Arjan couldn't deny that. "But you're my mate. We're meant to be together and nothing changes that."

"I know, but we live on opposite sides of the world to each other, Arjan. I can't just pack up my life and say goodbye to a career I love, simply because you believe we've got some kind of unbreakable bond."

Arjan almost punched the wall in frustration. He'd waited so long to have Kees back in his life, and now it seemed he was about to lose him all over again.

And whose fault is that? You pretty much drove him away before. How can you be surprised that this time he might want to go of his own free will?

Chapter Fifteen

After the drama that had surrounded the departures of Rob van Bergen and Eline Vos from Excelsior Systems, Kees needed an opportunity to forget about everything and have a good time. The Chaos Theory gig, he was sure, would provide that.

When he and Arjan arrived at the building that housed Hemel en Aarde, a queue of around twenty people already stood waiting to be let in. Unsure whether he and Arjan needed to join the back of the line, he walked up to the black-clad, thick-necked doorman, who clutched a clipboard and had a visible earpiece in his left ear.

"Hi," Kees addressed him uncertainly. "I should be on the guest list. Kees van der Veer, plus one."

The man ran a stubby finger down the typewritten list of names attached to his clipboard. Halfway down, he stopped and nodded. "Go through. The coat check is in the lobby, and the main hall and bar are down the stairs."

It being a fine night, neither man had bothered with a heavy coat, so they had no need to stop off and leave anything in the cloakroom. They descended the stairs and found themselves in a low-ceilinged room with a stage at one end, raised no more than a foot or so from the floor. To their left was a well-stocked bar, set away from the dance floor behind a sturdy wooden balustrade. A staircase led up to a balcony that would provide a decent vantage point for watching the action below. Though Chaos Theory wasn't due to perform for another half-hour, already the place was two-thirds full, with people having claimed the spots closest to the stage.

While Arjan went to the bar and ordered their drinks, Kees studied the mural that adorned the wall to his right. In keeping with the venue's name, 'Heaven and Earth', the unknown artist had painted a sequence of angels and demons, in a style that resembled a mediaeval triptych. But this was a very modern interpretation of the subject. The figures were overtly sexual, wearing very little other than the wings they wrapped around their own and each other's bodies. One portrait of a black-winged male demon with a naked man kneeling before him in some perverse act of worship had Kees' jeans growing tight around his crotch, and he was grateful when Arjan thrust a drink into his hand.

"What's this?" he asked. From the evidence of the glass-fronted fridges behind the bar, the venue stocked an extensive range of bottled beers, but Arjan had presented him with a glass of brown liquid in which ice cubes floated.

"Jack Daniel's and Coke. What else would you drink in a place like this?"

Kees tried to hide his surprise. Coming from Johnny, he would have expected such a sentiment, but not

Arjan. "You know, you sound just like a veteran rocker."

"That's because I am. Don't treat me as if all I listen to is the sentimental old songs my uncle used to sing. I was at the Paradiso the night Nirvana tore the place apart."

Now Kees couldn't prevent his jaw from gaping. That concert had become legendary, immortalized on an album released after Kurt Cobain's death. It had taken place in 1991, when Kees was ten and far too young to be able to attend. Arjan, on the other hand, would have been... He shook his head, not wanting to think about the obvious age gap between them. Arjan had said it didn't matter.

He took a swallow of his drink. Bourbon had never been his poison, but the sweetness of the cola masked its bite. "So, tell me what they were like? Nirvana, I mean. I'm so envious that you got to see them."

"They were amazing. So raw, so powerful. But you knew you were in the presence of a troubled soul..."

Around them, the room was filling up. From what Johnny had told Kees, apart from a couple of music journalists and bloggers who were friends of the band, everyone here was a member of the Chaos Theory fan club. Invitations had been issued to them alone, in a move designed to ensure only the hardcore fans who'd been following the band for years would be present at the gig.

By the time they'd finished their first drink and were halfway through their second, Kees felt a pleasant buzz. Any minute now, the band would take the stage and the air was already thick with anticipation.

"*Goedenavond*, Amsterdam!"

A roar went up from the crowd as Tyler stepped up to the microphone to address them in a mixture of

English and Dutch. Behind him, the other members of Chaos Theory were filing onstage. Chris settled behind the drum kit, and Dan, the rhythm guitarist, took up his place at the right of the stage. Johnny was pulling the strap of the bass that one of the roadies had tuned for him over his shoulder.

"It's great to see you all again," Tyler went on. "And it's great to know that word of this gig didn't leak out because you can all...keep it secret!"

With that, the band launched into *Keep It Secret*, a song from the first album Johnny had appeared on. It seemed to Kees that he, Arjan and a couple of men who leaned against the bar with the 'too cool for school' attitude that marked them out as journalists were the only ones not singing along. The fans right by the stage were nodding their heads wildly along to the music, and behind them seven or eight lads had formed a compact mosh pit, deliberately pushing and barging each other as they danced.

"They're good, aren't they?" Arjan's breath was hot against Kees' ear as he bent close to make sure he could be heard over the amplified music.

"Oh, yeah." Kees felt a strange swelling of pride at the thought that Arjan appreciated his best friend's talent. Chaos Theory might be influenced by the bands they had grown up listening to, like the Foo Fighters and Pearl Jam, but Tyler's haunting, melodic vocals and Johnny's clever lyrics gave them a voice that was all their own.

Arjan slipped an arm round him, letting his palm settle on Kees' firm arse cheek. Kees made no move to pull away. In the dimly lit room, no one would be able to see where Arjan's hand rested, and even if they could, this was Amsterdam — the city whose unofficial motto Kees had always thought was 'each to his own'.

For the next forty-five minutes, Chaos Theory played a selection of their biggest hits, throwing in a couple of new songs, which seemed to receive a generous reception from a crowd who had not heard them before tonight. Kees, warmed by alcohol and the steady presence of Arjan's hand on his butt, started to feel distinctly horny. It wasn't the time or the place, but he could only think of sliding to his knees in front of Arjan and placing his lover's dick in his mouth.

He was distracted from his rude daydreams by the sight of Johnny stepping up to his microphone. Until now, Tyler had been the one introducing the songs, but the reason why Johnny had taken the limelight soon became clear.

"We'd like to play a very special number for you now," he said. "As you know, Amsterdam lost one of its true icons a few days ago and in tribute to that man, the late, great Danny de Wit, we give you… *Stadt van mijn Hart.*"

City of my Heart. Everyone knew that song. It had been one of Danny de Wit's biggest hits, in the days when he had been a variety show crooner. A heartfelt celebration of Amsterdam and its people, the song was usually performed as a slow number designed to have the audience swaying along and belting out the words. The version Johnny sang was faster, more raucous, and it seemed every voice in the place was raised as he reached the chorus.

"Oh, beautiful city of my heart,
There's nowhere I'd rather be…"

"My God…"

Kees turned to see Arjan rooted to the spot, his expression unreadable. "Are you okay?"

"I don't know whether to laugh or cry." He appeared overwhelmed by the display of emotion all around him. "I mean... I know my uncle was popular, but I didn't expect this."

"It must be a great thing, to be loved like that," Kees mused. "To have an appeal that spans the generations..."

"Kees, stop philosophizing, please," Arjan ordered. "I think I need to be somewhere else."

"You want to leave? But we're supposed to be meeting up with Johnny after the gig."

"I know, and we will. But for now, I want you to come with me."

They pushed their way through the crowd to the back of the hall. Following the illuminated exit signs, they found themselves in a corridor. Even with the door closed, the thump of Johnny's bass still echoed.

The men's and women's toilets stood side by side. Arjan pushed open the door to the gents' and half-dragged Kees over the threshold in his haste to be inside.

The room, with its blue and white tiling and wooden stalls, was empty. Arjan pushed Kees up against the wall and gave him a fierce kiss.

"You're not thinking of—?" Kees felt his cock pulse as he realized why Arjan had brought him in here.

"Come on, Kees. Live a little. You can't tell me you're not up for this."

His lover knew him far too well. A quickie in the toilets of a music club had never been his style, but when Arjan suggested it, the thought had the blood pounding in his temples and his jeans straining to contain his rapidly swelling hard-on.

Arjan looked around, and spotted a vending machine on the wall at the side of the washbasins. As well as condoms, it contained something described as a 'pleasure kit'. A smile crossed his face as he rooted in his pocket and brought out a handful of coins.

"Now this will come in useful..." He fed the machine, and pulled out the tray at the bottom to retrieve his purchase. Then he guided Kees into one of the empty stalls, and locked the door behind them.

They shared a hot, tongue-twining kiss, their mouths mashed together as each fumbled to do undo the other's jeans. Once their clothing was around their ankles, Arjan ripped open the pleasure kit. Along with condoms and a couple of small sachets of lube, it contained a seashell pink and white plastic cock ring. As he examined it, he raised an eyebrow. The reason for his sardonic expression became clear when he flicked a switch on the little ring and a low hum filled the air.

"Interesting," Arjan murmured. "Now, bend over the cistern. We don't have a lot of time."

Kees did as he'd been told, clinging onto the cool porcelain and thrusting out his rump. The faint, artificially floral tang of disinfectant assailed his nostrils, but the surroundings were clean enough. He heard Arjan rip open one of the condoms and looked over his shoulder to watch the mundane action of his lover fitting the rubber in place, followed by the much more exciting sight of him sliding the stretchy cock ring down to the root of his shaft.

Arjan anointed Kees' arse with the lube, unable to take as long as he usually would, making sure the hole was open and slick. But the sheer rudeness of what they were doing had Kees welcoming the imminent penetration.

When Arjan pressed up close behind him, guiding the head of his dick to Kees' anal opening, he took a deep breath. He felt Arjan's plump crown, sheathed in latex, being pushed inside, and bore down to ease its entry. A brief, stinging discomfort quickly died away, to be replaced by a delicious feeling of fullness as his lover thrust further in. He didn't know whether it was due to the cock ring or just his imagination, but Arjan's length seemed bigger and thicker than he had ever known it.

"Okay?" Arjan muttered in his ear, once he was as deep as he could go. He held himself steady, gripping onto Kees' hips tightly.

Kees could distinctly feel the little plastic toy, trapped between his body and Arjan's. He could only grunt in reply, anticipating a style of pleasure he'd never before experienced. Arjan must have flicked the on-switch, because in the next instant, the ring started to buzz.

He had no idea how the pulsations must feel at Arjan's root, but they were being transmitted to the sensitive rim of his arse in delightful fashion. Normally, he'd have needed to wrap his own hand round his shaft and bring himself off while Arjan fucked him, but the wicked vibrator was creating more than enough in the way of stimulation.

Arjan thrust hard and fast, without finesse. His balls slapped against Kees' arse with every stroke, and he grunted with effort. Kees bit his lip. He wanted to vocalize his enjoyment but was too afraid that at any moment someone might walk into the toilets and hear what they were doing.

"Oh, Kees, your arse is so tight." Arjan groaned.

"Maybe it's just that your cock is so big," he responded. "And it's fucking me so well…"

They were the last words Kees managed to spit out before his orgasm overtook him, his cum splashing into the toilet bowl. Arjan followed seconds after, burying his mouth in Kees' neck as he came.

After such a frantic spending of bliss, all Kees could do was slump against the cistern, still aware of the ring vibrating against his flesh.

Arjan pulled out of his arse, and Kees dragged himself upright. He turned to see his lover switch off the toy and remove it from around his cock.

"It's funny," Arjan said as he disposed of his condom. "I always thought putting a ring on it meant you were making some kind of commitment."

Their eyes met. Kees was the first to look away. It might have been meant as a joke, but Arjan's comment had struck a chord. He couldn't deny that he wanted to take their relationship to the next level, but it just wasn't possible. How could anything serious develop when they lived in different countries? More than that, he feared that if he gave his heart to Arjan, as he could so easily do, he would only have it broken again.

"How much charge do you think there is left in that thing?" Kees asked, zipping himself back into his jeans.

Arjan examined it. "I don't know. Maybe there's some information in the packaging. But we're going to have fun finding out."

They finished dressing, then let themselves out of the toilet stall. As they emerged, the door opened and a young man in a black Chaos Theory T-shirt with its sleeves deliberately torn out entered the restroom. If he noticed that Kees and Arjan had left the same cubicle, he didn't say anything.

By the time they returned to the main hall, the band was playing *Hanging Fire*, their biggest hit and the song they usually saved for an encore. Finishing with a flurry of power chords on his guitar, Tyler placed the instrument close to the speaker so the crowd was treated to a howl of feedback, then he stepped back to the mic.

"Thanks, you've been a wonderful audience. Good night and take care, Amsterdam."

The stage lights were extinguished, and the band walked off. Despite a good couple of minutes' chanting for more from the audience, they did not return, and the main lights came up, signaling the end of the gig.

People began to filter out of the hall. Kees and Arjan made their way to the lip of the stage, Kees keeping an eye out for the band's manager, Grady, who he'd met at the concert in New York.

Grady was deep in conversation with one of the bar staff, but when he spotted Kees, he broke off to direct him and Arjan through a side door into the backstage area.

"The guys are in the Green Room," he informed them. "It's down the hall on the right."

A black-clad bouncer guarded the door to the room, barring their way, but when Kees explained who they were and that they'd spoken to Grady, the manager's name seemed to act as the password that allowed them inside.

"That was just amazing," Kees said, as he and Arjan joined the band. He'd expected the scene in the Green Room to be one of debauchery, with half-dressed groupies everywhere. Instead, Tyler, Chris and Dan drank from beer bottles, and tucked into the selection of cheeses and cured meats that had been left out for them.

Johnny caught Kees in a bear hug. "So glad you came. And you must be Arjan, right?"

Arjan nodded. "I really enjoyed the show. And thank you so much for the tribute to my uncle Danny. That meant a lot to me."

Johnny took a pace back. "Wow, Kees never said his boyfriend had a famous relative." He turned to his bandmates. "Hey, guys, this here is Danny de Wit's nephew."

Arjan appeared to be blushing, though Kees couldn't tell whether his embarrassment was caused by Johnny's gushing introduction or by the fact that he'd been referred to as his boyfriend. The relationship they had somehow seemed more important than that. On his part at least, he knew it would not be an exaggeration to say he was in love with Arjan, though he still wasn't willing to admit as much.

"So, Kees, it's nice to see you again. Arjan, good to meet you, buddy. Why don't you both grab yourselves a drink and then come tell us how awesome we were." Tyler grinned. Bare-chested and with sweat gleaming on his skin, he was obviously still on a high from performing on stage and his enthusiasm was infectious.

"Well, I've seen a fair few bands in my time, and it's no exaggeration to say you're up there with the best," Arjan said, helping himself to a bottle of beer and handing another to Kees. "And I'm so pleased you played *Blind*. That was always my favorite track off your first album, a really underrated song…"

Kees could tell the band members were impressed by Arjan's knowledge of their music. In truth, so was he. Every day he learned of something else they had in common. Maybe Arjan was right in his assertion that they were always meant to be together.

"I can see why you've got it so bad for this guy," Johnny murmured in Kees' ear. "He's definitely a keeper. I'm really happy for you, Kees."

"Thanks." He took a swig of his beer and looked over to where Arjan stood laughing and joking with Tyler. Happiness, as he knew all too well, was only temporary, and he couldn't help thinking that something would come along to snatch it away from him.

Chapter Sixteen

Kees let himself into the apartment, thinking that today he must really start looking into making his arrangements to go back to New York. He'd already checked his vacation allowance for the year and knew he had enough free days to allow him to stay here at least until the beginning of the following week. He tried not to think about the expression on Arjan's face when he'd said he was intending to leave Amsterdam, and he wished the situation could be otherwise, but his life was in the States now. Arjan would find someone else—maybe even someone of his own kind—who really understood what it was like to be able to shift their form at will. And he needed to leave soon, before his feelings for Arjan became so intense that he simply couldn't break away.

He switched on the TV and tuned to the local news. The lead story appeared to be the flash flooding that was causing serious disruption to the south of the city. A reporter, wearing wellingtons and a bright yellow raincoat, stood at the entrance to Amsterdam Zuid station, up to her calves in water.

He went to make himself a cup of coffee. When he returned to the living room, it was to see a familiar face on the screen behind the newsreader's head. He turned up the volume.

"Police have identified the woman stabbed in an attempted robbery at a jeweler's in De Clerqstraat as Lise de Wit, widow of—"

Kees tuned out for a moment, sickened by what he'd heard. Did Arjan know what had happened to Lise?

He forced himself to listen to the rest of the report.

"...hospital, where she is said to be in a stable condition. The shop's owner, Ton Molenaar, was pronounced dead at the scene. This is the third similar attack in the area in the last two months..."

Kees grabbed for his phone, but before he could dial out, it began to ring. When he answered it, Arjan's voice snapped, "The bastard tried to kill her, too, Kees. It's not enough that he murdered Danny..."

He could hear street noise in the background, the honking of horns and raised voices, and wondered where his lover was.

"Arjan, slow down. We don't know for sure that this is connected to Danny's death. I'm watching the report on TV, and it sounds like Lise was in the wrong place at the wrong time. It could all just be a coincidence."

"With De Jager, there are no coincidences." Arjan's tone was grim. "He'd have been watching her, making himself familiar with her movements, learning the best time to strike. And don't forget, he's very good at making murder look like an accident."

"But if that's the case, why would he kill the jeweler? He wasn't connected to the pride, was he?"

"No, and I don't think that was intentional. Either it was an attempt to make this look like a genuine robbery — attack the owner, as well as the client — or the man tried to protect my aunt and lost his own life in the process. All I know is that we need to go and see Lise, impress on her the need to get out of the city as soon as possible."

"But..."

"This is the first time De Jager has left someone alive. It's a mistake on his part and my guess is that at the next possible opportunity, he'll finish the job."

"So what are you going to do?"

"I'm at the taxi rank now. I'm on my way over to the hospital, in the Oosterpark. I'll see you there. And Kees..." Arjan paused. "Be careful."

* * * *

Half an hour later, Kees walked into the reception area of the big, modern hospital where Lise had been taken, on the east side of the city.

"I'm here to see Lise de Wit."

The receptionist consulted her computer before replying, "I'm sorry, *meneer. Mevrouw* de Wit is in intensive care, and visiting hours aren't until seven o'clock."

"The police are there with her, aren't they?"

When she didn't immediately deny the suggestion, Kees added, "Well, I have information regarding the case. It's very important that I speak to them."

The woman regarded him uncertainly, then said, "Very well. But please appreciate that the patient is very ill. Try not to upset her." Still clearly not sure that she was doing the right thing, she gave him instructions on how to reach the ICU.

Kees thanked her then dashed for the lift. It took him to the first floor, where he strode down the corridor toward the unit where Lise was being treated. He met a familiar figure coming in the other direction—the red-haired policeman who'd arrived late at the scene the night Danny de Wit had died.

The man nodded at Kees.

"Inspector—" Kees sought for his name, then recalled that they had never been properly introduced.

"De Roy. But please, call me Piet." He smiled, little creases appearing around his pale blue eyes, and took Kees' hand in a firm grip. "I'm just grabbing coffees while we wait for De Wit's widow to come round from the anesthetic." He lowered his voice. "The tip of the knife broke off when it hit her rib, according to the doctor. Very nasty, and suggests a man motivated by a great deal of rage. But at least she was luckier than the guy who owned the shop."

Kees wondered exactly how much Piet had seen. "Were you... Did you investigate the scene?"

The policeman shook his head. "No, but we gotten called in because of what happened to her husband. Personally, I don't see the connection, but something bad happens to both of them within the space of a couple of weeks... Obviously someone thinks it's suspicious." He snapped his fingers, as if a thought had just occurred to him. "By the way, when you gave your statement about the car that hit Danny de Wit, you said it was some kind of dark saloon, right? Well, a couple of officers on foot patrol found a burnt-out vehicle matching that general description in the underground car park just off Dam Square. The forensics team have been going over it, but they don't reckon they'll find much."

"Well, thanks for the update." Kees struggled to hide his disappointment at the lack of a breakthrough.

Piet shrugged. "No problem. Anyway, you go in and see *Mevrouw* de Wit. Your friend"—he didn't sound like he was angling for more information about the truth of Kees' relationship with Arjan—"is already here."

When Kees stepped into intensive care, it was to be greeted by a faint, antiseptic smell and the steady beeping of the machines to which Lise was connected. Piet's fellow Inspector, Sophie Engelen, paced the floor of the room, while Arjan sat in a chair by the hospital bed and a nurse fussed around Lise. Kees was relieved to realize that the patient had her eyes open, though the pallor of her face alarmed him.

"*Meneer* van der Veer," Inspector Engelen greeted him.

"How is she?" Kees asked anxiously. Though he barely knew Lise, he was concerned for her.

"She's conscious, but weak. The medical staff would very much prefer that we weren't here, so if you could keep it brief..."

"Of course."

He walked over to the bed, just in time to hear Arjan say, "Get away from here, Lise. Go stay with your family. This city is not safe for us right now."

In response, Lise muttered something Kees did not understand, and he assumed she spoke in her native Swedish. But from the way she clutched at Arjan's hand, Kees sensed she had taken heed of the warning.

Arjan rose from the chair. "Take care of yourself," he murmured to Lise. To Kees, he said, "We can go. I've told Inspector Engelen everything I know about what happened to my aunt, which is nothing." He shot a pointed look at Sophie, who did not respond.

Outside in the corridor, Kees said, "I spoke to that other policeman, Piet. He told me about Lise's injuries. It sounds pretty bad."

"Not bad enough, from De Jager's point of view. He wanted her dead, and she's lucky he didn't get his wish." He pulled his phone from his pocket. "I need to speak to Lise's parents. Let them know what's happened."

"Don't you think you're taking too much of this on your shoulders, Arjan?"

"Who else is going to do it? My father is getting too old, and half the pride still don't seem to believe they're in any kind of danger. But we're all at risk, and so are you." Fury blazed in Arjan's eyes. "Someone has to keep us all safe and stop De Jager before he attacks again. I intend to make sure that the only person living in fear around here is him."

Kees and Arjan made their way to the lift and waited for it to arrive. As the doors closed, Kees caught a glimpse of Piet de Roy standing watching them, a cup of coffee in each hand and that cocky little smile on his face. Despite all Arjan's concerns, Kees found the presence of the two inspectors reassuring. They would not allow anything bad to happen to Lise de Wit on their watch, and they would catch the man responsible for almost killing her. He only hoped that if the legend was true, and this was indeed the work of De Jager, that the police got to the man before Arjan did.

Chapter Seventeen

"I heard from Lise this morning," Arjan said.

Kees had come to the office to meet him, and now they were on their way to Amsterdam's most famous department store, De Bijenkorf, to buy a get-well present for Lise. At the height of the lunch hour, the city's main shopping streets were busy. Not the best time of day for making a purchase, but it was the only slot he'd had available in his schedule, and so they were braving the crowds of tourists.

"How is she?"

"Doing well. They just discharged her from hospital, and she's arranged to get a flight out to Schiphol tomorrow afternoon. She's going to be staying with my parents until then, so at least she heeded my advice about being somewhere she's not on her own."

"Have the police said anything more about the man who attacked her?" Kees asked.

"I haven't heard anything new from them, which leads me to assume they're no nearer to finding him."

"They told me the car they believe collided with Danny was found somewhere very close to here.

Seems like the guy who did it knew plenty about covering his tracks. And whoever stabbed Lise left a clue behind in the form of that bit of broken-off knife. But at least that might make it easier for them to find him." Kees brushed a windblown lock of hair from his face. "Maybe the police are right, and there really is no connection between the two cases."

It was an idea Arjan had considered at length, but he still couldn't shake his conviction that De Jager had been behind both crimes. "I didn't really discuss that when I spoke to Inspector Engelen. As I'm sure you can imagine, my aunt just wants to put the incident behind her."

They crossed the junction at Raadhuisstraat, scurrying before the lights changed and a tram started to move in their direction. When they came to Dam Square, instead of the usual street performers who dressed as some exotic sea god and the Grim Reaper and stood on plinths made from beer crates, they saw a small group of police attempting to hold back a number of noisy demonstrators.

"What's going on here?" Kees asked.

"Some kind of anti-capitalist protest, I believe," Arjan replied. "You know, the type of activists who complain about globalization and the evil influence of powerful corporations while simultaneously organizing these demos on their iPhones."

Kees grinned. "So I take it you don't approve of their message?"

"I'm not saying their arguments lack merit entirely. I've built Excelsior up from nothing, and I very much enjoy being a wealthy man. But I still have a civic duty to pay tax and help others, and I don't have a lot of time for those who think otherwise. You listen to some of these people, though, and I don't think they really have a clue what they want or who their grievances are against. I mean... I've even heard one of them saying their aim is to live in a world without money."

"What, so you'd...barter for goods?" Kees was clearly attempting to imagine how such a system would work. "Offer payment in kind for services rendered? Actually, that's not a bad idea. I won't ask for a fee for having found your saboteur. You can pay me with your body instead."

"If that's the case, I think I've already made a pretty good down payment..."

He stopped, aware that Kees was only half listening.

"Look, I'm sure I know that guy." Kees jabbed a finger in the direction of one of the protestors. "The one with the dreadlocks and the scarf pulled up to his nose. You see him?"

Arjan studied the man Kees indicated. He was ranting into a camera belonging to one of the local TV news crews. His blue eyes, almost the only part of his face that was not concealed, glittered with rage as he gestured to a placard held by a colleague. It read 'RIGHTS FOR ALL, NOT JUST THE ELITE'.

"Yeah, I do," he said. "And I recognize him, too. It's Eline's boyfriend, Simon. We saw him meet her outside the office, remember?"

"And now I think I can guess why she was passing the information onto him. It's not because she's afraid of him or because they're intending to siphon money into some account of their own or one belonging to that Wolf guy. This may sound stupid, but isn't it possible that if he's part of some group that wants to do away with all forms of currency, they'd want to get rid of the virtual stuff as well as the cold, hard cash?"

"It's not a conclusion I'd have jumped to before today," Arjan admitted, giving the suggestions some consideration, "but now you say it, it doesn't seem that unlikely. But it'll be the job of whoever prosecutes Eline to prove that, though we'll give them as much evidence as we can in support of the theory."

"Speaking of Eline, you don't see her anywhere, do you?"

Arjan glanced round quickly, before shaking his head. "No, but maybe we should get out of here, just in case. I don't think I'm her favorite person right now. I don't know about you, but I've gone off the idea of shopping."

"But what about a present for Lise? Isn't that why we're here, after all?"

"Let's go back to my apartment. We'll grab a couple of *broodjes* on the way. I can buy her something online and get it shipped out to her parents' place so she can enjoy it there."

They set off in the direction they'd come, leaving the protest behind. Even with a stop-off at a nearby café so they could pick up the filled rolls he'd suggested, along with two bottles of Coke, and a portion of creamy Greek yoghurt topped with honey and strawberries, they were at the house on Prinsengracht within fifteen minutes.

Arjan brought up the website for De Bijenkorf on his tablet and set about buying a lavish box of hand-made pralines for Lise, the perfect thing to appeal to her sweet tooth.

In the middle of this process, his phone buzzed, and he broke off to check the message. He looked up at Kees, who was munching on an egg salad *broodje*, with a wicked smirk. "Good news. The client I was supposed to be seeing at two has missed his flight. So I don't have to dash back to the office right away."

"Oh?" Kees had obviously picked up on the inflection in his voice. "And how exactly were you thinking of spending this unexpected free time?"

"Just give me a minute to complete this transaction and I'll show you."

With a couple of clicks of his mouse, the chocolates were paid for and on their way to Lise's parents' home in Stockholm.

When he looked up from the tablet screen, it was to see Kees walking toward him. The man had been busy while Arjan had been occupied with his online shopping. In one hand, he carried the plastic pot of yoghurt and strawberries, and in the other, he held a spoon. But it was the manner in which he'd dressed to serve dessert that captured Arjan's attention.

Or should that be undressed? Arjan couldn't wipe the smile from his face.

Kees wore an apron decorated with a pattern of blue and white Delft tiles — and nothing else. His erection tented out the fabric and when he bent to place the pot on the coffee table, he treated Arjan to a saucy view of his bare arse cheeks and the dark cleft between them. In response, Arjan felt his own cock perk up, and he reached down to make himself more comfortable in his suit trousers.

"Try a taste of this." Kees dipped one of the strawberries in the yoghurt, then held it to Arjan's lips. He sucked the creamy goo from it, before closing his teeth around its end in exaggeratedly slow fashion and biting down. All the while, he never broke eye contact with Kees.

They repeated the process with another strawberry, but this time Kees licked off the yoghurt, swirling his tongue over and around the ripe, red fruit before dabbing it into the pot for a second time and offering it to Arjan.

Arjan thought this was possibly the most erotic thing he'd ever done, the air tense with anticipation between them. He took one of the berries and simply held it between his teeth, encouraging Kees to bite it. Their lips were almost touching, and when they'd eaten the fruit, the only logical course of action was to kiss.

Kees broke away to unhook the strap of the apron from around his neck and unfasten the bow. He tossed the garment to one side, and Arjan gave a little smirk at the sight of the other man's dick standing up tight to his belly.

To Arjan's surprise, Kees scooped up a little of the yoghurt and painted his own hard little nipples with it. Arjan stuck out his tongue and began to lap it away with cat-like flicks. He tasted the sweetness of honey mingled with the salt of Kees' sweat, savoring the taste more than any dessert he'd ever enjoyed in a fancy restaurant.

"Why don't you get undressed?" Kees suggested, sticking one of his fingers in the pot before licking it clean, the action full of promise. "What happens next could get a little messy."

He went into the bathroom, only to return a moment later with one of the fluffy dove gray towels that had Arjan's initials embroidered in the corner, and waited for Arjan to finish stripping. Then he spread it out on the floor, and motioned his now-naked lover to lie down on it.

Arjan settled himself on his back, his blond locks spreading out around him as he did. He looked up to see Kees smiling down at him. The thick nap of the terrycloth was deliciously soft against Arjan's skin.

His cock was rock hard and awaiting Kees' attention. Kees drizzled a generous trail of yoghurt down his lower belly, over his balls and around the base of his shaft, then began to lick.

At first, he studiously ignored Arjan's straining erection, concentrating instead on his flat belly and mopping up any drips that had landed in Arjan's pubic hair. The circling motions of Kees' tongue over his skin were strangely relaxing, and Arjan closed his eyes, giving into the delightful sensation of receiving an oral bath.

Eventually, Kees moved his face till it hovered directly over Arjan's pelvis so he could suck at the delicate skin that covered his balls. As he lingered on the sensitive spot between the root of Arjan's dick and his arsehole, Arjan let out a noise that was somewhere between a whimper and a purr.

Just when Arjan thought he might explode from frustration, Kees took the tip of his cock between his lips and flicked it with the point of his tongue. He grasped Arjan's solid, pulsing length in cool fingers and set about eating up all the yoghurt that coated it. He alternately fed the crown into his mouth, where it visibly bulged out of his cheek. Then he licked down the shaft.

Arjan bit his lips, muttering to himself as he felt his balls tighten in preparation. His hips jerked and he was coming, spurts of semen hitting the back of Kees' throat.

They rolled into an embrace, Kees lying on top of Arjan. When they kissed, Arjan could taste himself, salty and sharp, overlaid with the tang of yoghurt.

"Good?" Kees murmured.

He nodded, feeling the urge to return the compliment. Having heaved himself to his knees, he picked up the pot from where Kees had left it at the side of the towel. "Lie down and let me show you just how good..."

Chapter Eighteen

Although it was only just gone nine in the morning, a queue was already building outside the entrance to the Rijksmuseum. Arjan and Kees joined the back of the line, knowing that most of these people would need the ticket counter. Arjan had bought tickets for both of them online the night before, a move designed to save them some time.

"So what is it exactly you want to show me?" Kees asked, as they strolled into the first of the newly refurbished exhibition halls.

"You'll see. And I can't believe that for someone who was born in Amsterdam, this is your first visit. Did you not even come here on a school trip?"

Kees shook his head. "I was very good at getting out of anything that might have involved culture, and I used to think museums were boring."

"Well, this one is anything but. Come with me."

He led the way up to the second floor, where the galleries containing works from the Seventeenth Century were housed. This had been Amsterdam's Golden Age, the height of Amsterdam's prosperity and influence as a world power, and its citizens had rushed to be immortalized in oils. Nowadays, Arjan assumed they'd all be taking selfies and posting status updates on social media sites. On balance, he thought he'd rather admire the works of art that hung on these walls.

Among those who had lined up to be painted were the members of the city's various trade organizations and civic bodies. The most famous of these was the painting that had come to be known as *The Night Watch* — Rembrandt's stunningly detailed depiction of the Militia Company of District II. But here also were the guilds of crossbowmen and drapers, prosperous merchants and city officials.

Arjan bypassed all of these in favor of a dark, gloomy-looking portrait of a group of soldiers. A dozen or so men, clad in matching black uniforms with tall hats and lace ruffs around their necks, clutched staffs and pikes, and stared out of the canvas with serious expressions. The artist's identity remained unknown, but he was believed to be one of Rembrandt's students.

"See the one second from the right?" Arjan pointed out a young man with a sandy-colored beard, who had taken up a position toward the back of the group.

"Mm-hm." Kees nodded. "He looks kind of familiar, but I don't know why."

"He's a de Wit." Arjan fought back a smirk as he watched Kees look from the portrait to him and back.

"Wow, now you point it out, I can definitely see a resemblance. But I thought you told me you had to keep a low profile."

"We did. You won't see our faces among the spice merchants and the ranks of politicians. But there were so many militia groups, it was inevitable that at least one of them would come to contain a pride member. And he could quite easily have been fighting alongside people who had no idea about his real identity. Now..."

The sound of his phone ringing brought a guilty flush to Arjan's face. Even though phones were permitted in the exhibit halls, etiquette demanded that he should have put his on silent mode. He went to turn it to voicemail, intending to listen to the message and return the call when they left the museum, then stopped when he realized his mother was calling.

"Hey, Mama." He kept his voice low, glancing round to make sure he had not earned the ire of anyone admiring the nearby sculptures. "I'm sorry, but I can't really talk right now. Let me call you back when..."

Her response was rushed, tearful. "Arjan, *lieveling*, you need to come over right away. It's your father..."

* * * *

Arjan almost threw the fare into the taxi driver's hands in his haste to enter the de Wit family home. Never patient at the best of times, he had spent most of the journey willing the traffic to move faster as he'd considered all the terrible things that could have happened to his father. He hadn't waited for his mother to tell him what was wrong. The tone of her voice had been enough to have him dashing out of the museum after only the briefest of apologies to Kees.

Of course, Kees had offered to come with him, but this was something he had to do alone. If Cornelis had been murdered by De Jager—and what other explanation could there be?—then he didn't want Kees to see him break down.

He hammered on the front door of the grand house on Apollolaan, one of the most sought-after addresses in this part of the city. The four-bedroom property, with its striking red brick façade and steeply sloping roof, was a sign of how well the de Wits had done for themselves. Not just Danny, but Cornelis, too, had become mainstays of the community, in a way that would never have been possible in previous centuries. But none of that mattered. Not if De Jager had killed the head of the pride.

The Filipina maid, Nenette, answered the door. She greeted him with a wide smile, as if nothing was wrong. To Arjan, that didn't make sense. Nenette had been with the family for over twenty-five years, and she adored both of his parents. Why wasn't she more upset?

"*Meneer* Arjan. Come in. Your father is upstairs in his bedroom."

"Nenette, what's going on here? My mother said —" He broke off. Actually, his mother hadn't said anything. He hadn't given her the opportunity and had simply allowed his mind to fill in the blanks.

The maid just shook her head, and made a sweeping gesture with her hands, ushering him toward the stairs. "You go. I'll make you some coffee, bring it up to you."

He climbed the two flights up to the master bedroom. The door was ajar, and he knocked gently before entering. He walked in to see Cornelis sitting upright in his pajamas, his back supported by a number of pillows. The man's complexion looked sallow, and there were dark circles under his eyes, but otherwise he appeared to be in perfect health.

"My boy…"

Arjan looked from his father to his mother, who sat on a chair at her husband's bedside, then back. "What's going on? I thought you were—"

"Dead?" Cornelis gave a weak smile. "No, it'll take more than a simple cardiac event to kill me."

"Mama, what's he talking about? You were so upset…"

"Yes, and I'm sorry about that. I went into your father's study and found him lying on the floor, not moving. I panicked, called Doctor van Wijngaarden, but while I was waiting for him to arrive, Cornelis had already come round. The doctor examined him, and it seems he had a very small heart attack."

"Very odd," Cornelis chipped in. "Not at all the gripping pain I expected. More like a rather bad case of indigestion. But the next thing I knew, I'd blacked out."

Arjan wondered whether the unique metabolism of the pride members meant Cornelis had suffered such a minor reaction to a major event, or if many of the aches and pains men of a certain age experienced were actually linked to heart disease. Still, he was sure his father had received the most appropriate treatment— he might change doctors every few years, before any of them could begin to question his unusual longevity, but he always went for the best.

At the sound of a light rapping on the door, Arjan looked over to see Nenette attempting to enter the bedroom with a tea tray. He went and took the tray from her, then set it on the bedside table. She offered him a little smile of gratitude then retreated from the room, no doubt sensing that the family wished to be left in peace.

"But you're okay?" Arjan asked Cornelis, passing a cup of coffee to him.

"As fit as can be expected. Doctor van Wijngaarden says I need to take it easy for a couple of weeks—no strenuous exercise, no over-exciting myself, and alcohol only in moderation. And he wants me to cut down on the red meat." His father grinned, showing his sharp canine teeth, then took a sip of his drink. "As if that's going to happen."

Arjan added a splash of milk to his own coffee. "Well, I'm sure Mama will keep a close eye on you." He wanted to ask his parents not to scare him like this again, but he couldn't. He'd done a pretty good job of scaring himself, so obsessed with De Jager that he'd never stopped to consider a more mundane threat to his father's wellbeing.

"Of course. But this has set me thinking, you know." Cornelis patted the bedcovers by his side, encouraging Arjan to perch on the bed. "We all think we're going to live forever, and God willing, I've got another thirty good years ahead of me. But I need to look to the future. What if I were to have another...event like this? Something more serious, that left me incapacitated."

"Not you, Papa. You're as strong as an ox." Arjan's tone was reassuring, but he knew his father was right. A stroke, a fall, an acute bout of pneumonia... Shifters might recover from illness and injury much faster than humans did, but they weren't immortal. And severe trauma would finish them off just as swiftly and surely as anyone else.

"That may well be, but I've always known that the time would come when I have to step aside—let a younger man make the decisions, keep the stability of the pride intact."

"So why are you telling me this?"

"Because I've been considering all the potential candidates to take over, and there is no one I trust, no one I wish to see in charge more than you."

Arjan gaped at Cornelis in disbelief. "You... You can't be serious. I'm a virtual exile from the pride and have been ever since you found out I had a boyfriend." He didn't need to elaborate. Even after all these years, he could still remember the look on his parents' faces when they'd come home early from some function or other and caught him on the sofa in the living room with Paul, half undressed and locked in a passionate smooch. It hadn't mattered that both of them had been well over the age of consent or were taking all the necessary precautions. Cornelis and Betje de Wit had had plans for their son, and none of them had involved him ending up in a committed relationship with another man.

"That doesn't have to be an issue anymore," Cornelis said. "The pride has always had its rules, but we may have been too hard on you. Circumstances alter, and if you are right, and we are being targeted by the families again, then I need someone as strong and decisive as you to take charge of the situation."

He wanted to ask what had changed since they'd spoken at the airport hotel, when his father had been all too adamant that Arjan's concern about De Jager had been little more than paranoia. But he kept his counsel, knowing how much it must have cost Cornelis personally to come to this decision.

"Please, Arjan, think about it. I'm willing to step aside for you whenever you're ready to take on the role."

"And what about the rest of the pride? What will they have to say, especially Kaspar?" It was no secret that Arjan's second cousin, Kaspar, had ambitions to lead the pride.

"Kaspar's a fine young man, but he's wayward. He needs guidance. You could provide that for him."

"I don't know…"

"I'm not asking for a decision right this moment. But don't keep me waiting too long. If you're right in what you're saying, we may need to act fast when the time comes to face down De Jager."

* * * *

When Arjan left the house, half an hour later, he was in no less of an agitated a mood than when he'd arrived. But now his mind raced for very different reasons. He'd given up all thought of becoming pride leader a very long time ago, and now his father was asking him to take on the role he had believed would never be his.

He wanted to say yes, sure that in time he could win round all those who would be initially resistant to the thought of having him in charge. But he couldn't get past the biggest stumbling block of all, his relationship with Kees.

Try as he might, Arjan couldn't see anyone accepting that he had chosen a human as his mate. And if he had to choose between leadership of the pride and the man he loved…

He almost stumbled over his own feet. He'd never used the word 'love' in relation to his feelings for Kees, but there was no other way to describe it. He loved Kees van der Veer, and he would do anything to keep him from harm. But how could he turn his back on the needs of the pride at the time when they too were most in need of his protection?

The tram that would take him back into the center of Amsterdam appeared in the distance, and he broke into a jog to make sure he would reach the stop before it did. He spent most of the short journey back to the Prinsengracht mulling over his dilemma, and still he was no closer to finding a solution.

As he approached the *eetcafé* on the corner of his block, all other considerations were wiped from his mind. He could smell Kees' scent, lingering faintly on the breeze. His lover had been here recently. But he hadn't let himself into the apartment, as Arjan had asked him to do when he'd finished his tour of the Rijksmuseum. Instead, the spoor moved on down the canal. And what concerned Arjan was not the presence of the scent itself, but the top notes it contained — fear and adrenaline. Everything suggested that something had happened here, something that had caused Kees to flee in panic.

A drop of water splashed against his cheek, and Arjan looked up at the lowering sky. Rain would dilute the trail. He needed to move before the bad weather set in and it was washed away entirely. Following his nose, he set off in search of Kees.

Chapter Nineteen

An hour earlier...

Kees walked out through the main entrance of the Rijksmuseum and into a May morning that had grown unseasonably chilly. He hoped everything was okay with Arjan's father. The look of distress on the shifter's face as he'd explained that he had to leave and would see Kees back at the house on the Prinsengracht had been upsetting. But, he reassured himself, if something awful had happened, he'd have been in touch. *If De Jager turns out to have struck again, I'd know about it by now.* He wouldn't just have left me to wander round here on my own.

He decided that he'd go to the apartment, as agreed. If Arjan wasn't there when he arrived, he'd ring him and find out what was happening. He'd gained the impression that father and son had a somewhat strained relationship, but the manner in which Arjan had gone dashing off suggested he did care about the old man.

On the way, he stopped off at a baker's to pick up some hot sausage rolls. They'd had a snatched breakfast of bread, cheese and hard-boiled eggs before setting off to the museum, and now he was more than ready for something to eat. Maybe he and Arjan could take the rest of the bottle of red wine they'd opened last night to bed, and spend the afternoon having down and dirty sex.

Kees was still wrapped up in thoughts of their bodies entwining on Arjan's king-sized bed as he stood on the front step, searching in his pocket for the key. Arjan had given him a spare copy so he could come and go as he pleased, though he still preferred to spend time in his own apartment when he needed to concentrate on work.

The sound of shuffling footsteps came from behind him and he half turned, just as a man reached out to grab him from behind. Kees caught a glimpse of a figure with a hood pulled low over his brow and a scarf covering the bottom half of his face. He gained an impression of cold blue eyes, filled with hatred. More alarmingly, the flash of what appeared to be a knife blade glittered in his eye line, as his assailant brought his arm down in a sweeping arc.

Mind filled with thoughts of the attack on Lise de Wit in the jeweler's shop, Kees reacted in the only way he could, pushing at the man's chest to send him staggering back down the steps to land in an untidy heap on the floor. Then he was off, still clutching the brown paper bag to his chest. He had no idea where he was going, only that he needed to put as much distance as he could between himself and the knifeman.

Kees dashed along the narrow pavement, weaving in and out of groups of tourists sauntering in the opposite direction, and more than once running the risk of being hit from behind by a cyclist. When he looked back to see if he was still being followed, he thought he could see the hooded man pushing his way through a crowd, waiting to cross the road. He didn't take a second glance to make sure, just kept running until · he reached the junction with Prinsenstraat. Turn right, and he'd be back at his own apartment. This would all be over.

Some instinct, however, warned him against returning to his home. If he was being followed, he didn't want to run the slightest risk of his attacker discovering where he lived. He needed sanctuary and to see a friendly face. And so he carried straight on, until he hit the Brouwersgracht.

No longer thinking about the consequences of his actions, he crossed the gangplank of Johnny's houseboat in a couple of steps and banged hard on the door. "Please be at home," he muttered under his breath. "Please…"

"Okay, okay. Just hang on a minute…" came a mildly irritated voice from within.

Johnny pulled open the door, and stared at Kees. "Hey, man, is everything all right? You look awful."

"I got attacked," Kees managed between harsh, panting breaths. "Someone jumped me on the doorstep. Had a knife…"

"What the f—" Johnny ushered Kees into his home. "Come in. Sit down. Let me get you a glass of water and you can tell me about it."

Kees slumped heavily on the couch, feeling his heart rate slowly return to something approaching normal. "I need to spend more time in the gym," he muttered, gratefully accepting a drink from his friend. "Guess

I'm not as fit as I thought I was." He held out the grease-spotted paper bag to Johnny. "Sausage roll?"

"Thanks." Johnny took a seat at the side of him. "So, you're saying someone tried to mug you? Is that right?"

"I don't know. I just felt him grab me and when I saw he was armed, I got the hell out of there. I was so scared."

"And this was at your place?" He took a bite out of his snack and chewed, wiping flecks of pastry from where they tumbled into his lap.

"No. It's a complicated story. Arjan and I had gone down to the Rijksmuseum, only he got a call from his mother, telling him he was needed at home. There's some situation with his dad that I haven't got to the bottom of yet. So when I left the museum, I went up to Arjan's place to meet him there, like we'd arranged, and that's when I was attacked."

"And where's Arjan now?"

"I don't know. I haven't heard from him. Maybe I should give him a ring…"

At that moment, his phone buzzed. When he checked it, he saw a text from Arjan.

Where are you? I lost your scent near Prinsenstraat.

Knowing some things were better left unexplained, he decided against sharing the message with Johnny. Instead, he dialed Arjan's number.

"Kees, what's happening? Are you all right?"

"Yes. I'm at Johnny's. He's on the Brouwersgracht. The burgundy houseboat with the fake flamingo…"

"I'll be there in a couple of minutes." Arjan cut the call.

"He's on his way here. I hope you don't mind," Kees said to Johnny.

"Not at all. Like I told you the other night, the guy's cool. I think you two make a great couple." He finished his sausage roll, then dabbed at his lips with a napkin.

"Before he gets here, there's something I think I should tell you, but this is just between us, okay?"

"Of course." Johnny placed his hand to his heart. "You can trust me."

"You know Arjan's uncle was killed a couple of weeks ago. Well, his wife was attacked, too, in a robbery that went wrong on de Clerqstraat."

"Yeah, I saw something about that on the news. The family's having some rotten luck, wouldn't you say?"

You could put it like that. "Arjan seems to think that he might be next — and that I'm in danger, too."

"And you think that what happened just now…?"

"Well, it could be a coincidence. Like you say, just a random mugging. But Arjan isn't very big on coincidences." Kees was startled by a knock at the door. "Anyway, I'd be grateful if you didn't let him know I mentioned this."

Johnny said nothing, but gave Kees a look as if to say 'I've got your back'. Then he went to let Arjan in.

"Hi, Johnny." Arjan strode in. It seemed to Kees that he filled all the available space in the low-ceilinged room. "How's it going?"

"Not bad. Kees told me some guy tried to mug him outside your home."

"Really? Kees…"

"I'm fine, honestly. I came here because I didn't want to be on my own."

"Well, you did the right thing," Arjan assured him, though Kees sensed that he already knew there was more to the story than he'd been told. "Have you spoken to the police?"

"No, but I will. I'd just like to stay here a bit longer, collect my thoughts, if that's okay with you?" Kees addressed his appeal to Johnny.

"Well, to be honest, I'm expecting the rest of the band any time now. I thought it was them when you showed up. We're off to Wisseloord—got an all-night session booked."

For the first time, Kees noticed Johnny's bass guitar, propped up against the arm of the couch in its protective case.

"Tell you what," Johnny continued, "why don't the two of you come over to the studio with us and hang out for a while?"

Kees looked over at Arjan. Part of him thought it would be fun to spend time with the band, listening to them work on their new album. Then his thoughts flashed back to the man who'd attacked him, the icy hatred in his eyes, and he shivered.

Arjan, who must have sensed his unease, stepped in to speak on his behalf. "Thanks for the offer, Johnny, but I think Kees just needs some peace and quiet right now."

"Hey, don't worry about it. If you want to hang around here for a while, that's fine. There's beer in the fridge, or a bottle of vodka on the kitchen counter if you need anything stronger, so just help yourself." He pulled a key fob out of his pocket, slipped one of the keys off it and handed it to Kees. "That's so you can lock up when you go. Just leave it under the mat when you're done with it."

"Thanks." Kees rubbed the door key between his fingers as though it was some kind of talisman. "And you'll have to come over to mine before I go back to New York and I'll cook you dinner."

"I'll hold you to that." Before Johnny could add anything else, someone rapped at the door. He went to answer it, and when he returned, he had Tyler, Dan and Chris with him.

Kees had time to do little more than acknowledge the three men before Johnny had snatched up his bass and they were on the way out. He wondered what story his friend might spin to explain why he and Arjan had remained behind on the houseboat.

"So," Arjan said once they were alone, "tell me what really happened. Or do you honestly expect me to believe someone was only after your wallet?"

"Let me just take Johnny up on his offer of a drink, and then we'll talk." He went into the kitchen, found the bottle of vodka and two heavy-bottomed glasses, then poured himself and Arjan a shot. When he brought the drinks back into the living room, he took a seat and sat cradling his glass between his palms.

"Okay," he began. "What happened is that I was letting myself into your building, and someone grabbed me from behind. I was scared, and I ran. And like I told Johnny, it could have been a robber, but... I thought I recognized him."

"Really?" Arjan's eyes blazed with some emotion Kees didn't recognize, and a restless energy emanated from him, as if the urge to shift had overtaken him.

"He had his face covered, but there was something in his eyes." Kees took a sip of the vodka, relishing the warming feeling it sent through him. "I don't know for sure, but I keep thinking it could have been Eline Vos' boyfriend, Simon. I mean, he'd certainly be mad enough to pull a knife on either of us, after everything that's happened."

"It's possible, I suppose." Arjan appeared to be considering the theory Kees had put forward. "But you had the feeling it was someone you knew."

Somehow, that thought seemed to wipe away much of the strain surrounding Arjan. Kees no longer felt as though he might be confronted by a tense, growling lion at any moment.

"Yes. Wait, you were expecting me to say I'd been attacked by De Jager, weren't you?"

Arjan nodded. "It had crossed my mind, yes."

"Well, that's not possible, so you can stop worrying about it. Like I told the police, I never got a proper look at whoever was driving the car that hit Danny."

"Wasn't Lise supposed to be providing a description of the man who stabbed her to the police, so they could produce an e-fit?" Arjan persisted.

"Yes, and I'm sure that's been circulated, but I haven't seen it. Look, Arjan, I'm not blind to the fact that someone is out there killing members of the pride, but maybe your concern that I might be at risk from him is misplaced. There are other people who have reason to cause me—and you—more immediate harm, and maybe we should be considering that possibility." He sighed. "What have we got ourselves into, Arjan?"

"Nothing we can't handle." Arjan came to sit beside Kees and reached for his hand.

Again, Kees felt the powerful connection between them. With Arjan, he felt protected, even loved. Not that the shifter had ever used the word, but Kees was pretty certain from the way Arjan looked at him sometimes that it was how he felt.

He dropped a kiss on Arjan's cheek. "You really don't need to look after me all the time, you know. I've been doing a good enough job of it myself since I was eighteen."

"I'm aware of that." Arjan sounded solemn. "But when I caught your scent outside my home, and smelled the fear coming off you, I had to do something. I really couldn't bear to lose you, Kees..."

Kees stopped any more talk with another kiss, pressing his mouth to Arjan's. The shock of those terrifying moments when he'd fled from his assailant had passed, but adrenaline still fizzed through his veins.

He reached for Arjan's heavy silver belt buckle, murmuring, "God, I need you so much right now."

Arjan put out a restraining hand. He looked at their surroundings, at the general clutter of Johnny's daily life. "Are you quite sure you want to abuse your friend's hospitality like this?"

"Johnny won't mind. Believe me. And if he knew what we were doing, I'm sure he'd approve." He freed his fingers from Arjan's gentle grip and began to work on the other man's belt. "Like he said, he won't be back till tomorrow. No one's going to disturb us, so just enjoy this..."

He set about stripping Arjan, removing his boots before pulling off his jeans. The shifter had chosen not to wear underwear that day, and Kees had a moment's struggle to maneuver the denim down over the jutting length of his cock. Arjan's washed-out blue T-shirt and thick white socks he left in place, just because he liked the sight of him half-dressed. It made what they were about to do seem even more illicit, somehow.

Aware that his every moment was watched intently, he took off his own clothes then kicked off his muddied trainers. Naked, he got on the floor between Arjan's legs, the painted boards hard against his knees. He felt the houseboat swaying gently, rocked by the faint wash of some passing vessel, and wondered how long it would take him to get used to living on the water.

Gripping Arjan's shaft by its base, he dipped his head and lapped over the exposed helmet with flat sweeps of his tongue. The motion drew a slow hiss of pleasure from his lover, and when Kees glanced up, he saw that Arjan's eyes were half closed. Any qualms the man had about their fucking in Johnny's home had clearly been pushed away.

Slowly, Kees worshiped Arjan with his mouth, licking up and down the hard column of flesh. He took as much of it into his throat as he could, taking steady breaths through his nose and delighting in the audible groans that were the result of his actions.

As good as it would have been to keep on sucking Arjan till he came, he needed more. Kees wanted that thick, vital cock buried deeply in his arse. He let it slip from between his lips and went to retrieve a condom from his wallet.

He tossed the condom to Arjan, telling him to put it on. In the absence of lube, Kees improvised by spitting onto his fingers and using that to wet his own hole, a move he knew was sure to excite his already highly aroused lover even further. Then he gave Arjan's cock another lick, grimacing at the taste of the latex.

When Arjan made to rise from the couch, Kees shook his head, wanting to try something different. He straddled Arjan's thighs, and moved so that the head of the man's dick butted against his arsehole. Fixing his gaze with Arjan's, he sank down. He groaned at the sweetness of the feeling as he was stretched almost unbearably wide.

He linked his hands around the back of Arjan's neck and just sat for a moment, accustoming himself to the unusual angle of penetration. In his mind, sex was always best when he could look into his lover's eyes, and this position allowed him to do just that.

The houseboat moved again, just a little, and Kees seemed to feel the motion being transmitted through Arjan's shaft into his tight passage. It might be a fanciful notion, but it only served to emphasize the way they were joined, body and soul.

Then Arjan gave a slight thrust of his hips, breaking Kees' reverie. *Typical. Even when I'm on top, he's still the one setting the pace.* But Kees didn't object. He began to move with Arjan, the two of them finding a rhythm that soon built in pace and intensity.

Johnny's couch creaked alarmingly beneath them, and Kees momentarily wondered how he would explain to his best friend that they'd wrecked a piece of his furniture in the throes of passion. But it held firm, even as they moaned and gasped and rocked against each other.

Arjan howled out, and gave one last hard jab up into Kees' arse. Kees clung to his lover with one hand, pressing his fingers at the soft cotton of the faded T-shirt. With the other, he gave his length half a dozen quick tugs, enough to send cum shooting out to land on Arjan's taut, bare thigh.

Weak from the force of the orgasm that had ripped through him, Kees climbed off Arjan and curled up on the couch, resting his head on his lover's shoulder.

"I don't know about you, but I fancy another vodka," he said when he'd recovered his voice.

Arjan grunted and gave a nod of agreement. Kees got up, put on his T-shirt then took their glasses into the little kitchen. The bottle was almost empty, and he made a mental note to treat Johnny to a replacement as thanks for providing a refuge when he'd been most in need of one.

The danger had passed—for the time, at least. Looking out into the living room, where Arjan, sleepy and sated, waited on the couch, he couldn't help thinking the two of them still had their greatest threat to face before all this was done.

Chapter Twenty

Arjan closed down the file he'd been working on. With the police now officially involved in the investigation into Eline Vos' activities, he needed to collate all the data Kees had collected so he could pass it on both to them and to his own lawyers. There were still gaps—they had not yet been able to discover the real identity of Wolf, the anti-capitalist activist, but as far as Arjan was concerned, that was the police's job. They had officers devoted to monitoring a number of potentially disruptive groups, from the extreme fringe of the squatters' movement to the football hooligans who followed Ajax. He knew they would eventually turn up the information.

He tapped his watch face, wondering how most of the day had managed to slip away. He and Kees had made plans to have dinner at Kristof's, where he hoped to persuade Kees not to return to New York. Knowing his father wanted him to take on leadership of the pride had made Arjan begin to examine his priorities. Even with all the criminal behavior that had bedeviled the cryptocurrency project, he still believed he owned a strong, healthy business, and was proud of what he'd achieved in his career. But hand in hand with that went a growing desire to be settled in his personal life.

His parents at last appeared to have accepted that his attraction to other men meant he would never produce the grandchildren they'd always hoped for. Arjan didn't know how they'd react when they discovered his chosen mate was human—but when they met Kees, he was sure they'd come to love him.

As for the sex, Kees roused his deepest passions and gave him free rein to explore the kinky fantasies he'd not felt comfortable sharing with anyone else. He'd never done anything as reckless as having sex in the toilets at Hemel en Aarde since—well, since he'd made the decision to seduce Kees at that party so many years ago.

If only Kees didn't seem so set on throwing away all they had in pursuit of his own career. They hadn't talked much about what had happened with the so-called mugging, but the other afternoon, on the houseboat, they'd both come as close as they ever had to admitting the real strength of their feelings for each other. But when Arjan had tried to bring the subject up again, Kees had simply clammed up, as though he'd reached a threshold he didn't want to cross.

It was possible to make a long-distance relationship work, but Arjan didn't want the Atlantic to divide them. The intense bursts of passion on the rare occasions when they got together would not be enough to sustain him throughout those long, lonely stretches apart. Call him greedy, but he wanted Kees in his bed every night, wanted to spend the rest of his life with him, and he was prepared to do whatever it took to make him see that.

His phone buzzed, and he saw that he'd had a text from Kees. He stared at the message in growing disbelief.

Inspector de Roy is coming over to the apartment. He says he has news. Will call you as soon as I'm free.

A sick chill ran through him as he read the words again. Why was he only now learning the policeman's surname? Such an innocent piece of information, yet it held the key to everything that had happened since Anneke's body had been found, surrounded by all the necessary paraphernalia for injecting heroin.

Five hundred years ago, six families had gathered and sworn to rid Amsterdam of the pride. Arjan had learned the names of those families at his mother's knee, reciting them like a litany. Six surnames to treat with fear and suspicion. Schoonhoven, Van der Helst, Stoffels, Rendorp, Willemsen, de Roy...

All this time, his enemy had been closer than he had ever imagined, offering assistance, keeping him informed on the threat to his family—swearing that he would not cease in his efforts till this was over. Well, the cunning, devious bastard had led both him and Kees right into his trap.

Not even bothering to collect his jacket from where it hung on the back of his chair, he dashed from his office. He had to get over to Kees' apartment. He could only pray he wouldn't be too late.

* * * *

Arriving at the chemist's shop on Herenstraat, breathless from running all the way from the Excelsior offices, Arjan fumbled a set of keys from his pocket.

He held the spares to the main door and Kees' apartment. Kees had probably been in serious violation of his tenancy agreement by giving them to Arjan, but right now, that act could save his life.

He let himself inside. Nothing seemed amiss in the narrow stairwell, no signs of a struggle. *No surprises there.* Kees would have had no reason to suspect the man who'd come to visit was De Jager and would have welcomed him willingly.

Arjan took the stairs in cautious fashion. When he reached Kees' door, it was firmly shut. The beast within him yearned to break it down, but he had to suppress the urge. This was no time to let his baser instinct take over.

He turned the key in the lock and crept inside, to be greeted by a sight that drove all thoughts of adopting a restrained approach from his mind.

Kees struggled in the firm grip of Piet de Roy, his eyes wide with terror. The policeman held a long-bladed knife to his throat, pressing it against the skin. Arjan's hackles rose. Already, there was a trail of bright red blood oozing down Kees' neck.

"And here he is. The real star of the show. So glad you could join us, Arjan." De Roy spoke in a mocking tone. "You're just in time to watch me slit your lover's throat."

Arjan didn't stop to issue a plea for de Roy to halt his actions or to beg for Kees' life. Confronted by the bastard who had already killed three of his pride and who now intended to butcher the man he loved above all others, reason and rationality fled. The need to shift that gripped him became too much to resist. Even as he launched himself at de Roy, he was changing, letting his inner lion loose.

Kees had managed to wriggle free, as De Jager was presented—for the first time, if his awestruck expression was any indication—with the sight of his prey in its animal form. His momentary hesitation allowed Arjan to spring. He clamped his teeth tight around the man's throat, feeling flesh and bone tear beneath his assault. Then pain bloomed in his shoulder, hot as fire, and he fell back, howling in agony as he turned back from beast to man.

Chapter Twenty-One

In the days that followed the fatal encounter in Arjan's apartment, Kees could only recall what had happened as a series of snapshots. It was as though his mind had sought to protect him from the full horror of Piet de Roy's death. He remembered coming to and seeing the man sprawled on the floor, a gaping, red wound where his throat had been and his blue eyes staring up sightlessly, their cold light dimmed. Arjan huddled beside the body, naked, his clothes in shreds around him and blood flowing from the flesh wound on his shoulders.

How they'd explained away the bizarre details of what had happened to the police, he could never quite say. Somehow, though, Inspector Engelen — a woman who Kees knew would brook no nonsense — seemed to accept that Arjan had acted in self-defense after her colleague had turned a gun on him.

Though Arjan had been hit by a bullet, he'd been lucky. It had done little more than graze his flesh. He'd been kept in the hospital overnight as a precaution, but with his accelerated healing powers, after a couple of days all that remained was a puckering scar that he would retain as a souvenir of his and Kees' brush with death.

He still couldn't believe how easily he'd been manipulated by De Jager. Of all the people who might have been responsible for murdering three members of Arjan's pride—as well as making a failed attempt on Lise de Wit's life—he would never have dreamed it could be a member of the Amsterdam police force.

The details of the moments up to Arjan's transformation remained much clearer in his memory. When he'd let Piet into the apartment, he'd been expecting to be asked to confirm some detail of the statement he'd given in the wake of Danny's fatal accident. But things had played out in a very different fashion.

* * * *

Three days earlier…

"Inspector de Roy, please do come in." Kees led the way up the stairs to his apartment. "I hope I can be of assistance with whatever this is all about. You were a little vague in your phone call."

"Don't worry. I'll explain once we're upstairs." The detective climbed the winding steps with broad strides. He seemed to buzz with energy, as if he had information he couldn't wait to impart.

"Well, this is impressive," he commented as they walked into the living room.

Kees tried to see his temporary home through the visitor's eyes. He'd grown very fond of it, from the striking mural of a dandelion clock, its fluffy seeds blowing through the air, which took up one wall to the compact kitchen where he'd brewed so many pots of coffee in the past few weeks.

"The company I work for found it for me," he replied. "I'll be sad to leave it when I go."

"Oh, you're leaving us, are you?" Piet sounded surprised.

"Yes, I can't remember whether I told you, but I'm here on business. I've completed what I came here to do, and I'll be on my way back to New York in a few days."

"Then we need to do this now."

Something in the policeman's tone sounded a little odd to Kees, but he didn't think anything of it. If the police needed to contact him again, he'd be sure to leave them all the details of where they could find him.

"Can I get you something to drink? Coffee? Tea?"

"A glass of water will be fine, thank you."

Kees went over to the kitchen counter and began to fill a glass with the chilled water he kept in the fridge. Suddenly, he was grabbed by the throat and around the waist.

"What the—?" Kees croaked, trying to break free from Piet's grip. The glass fell from his fingers and landed on the floor, shattering as it did.

Piet loosened his hold on Kees' windpipe. From out of the corner of his eye, Kees caught sight of him reaching to take the cook's knife from the magnetic rack on which it was held.

"This will be a tragic accident," Piet murmured in his ear. "You came home to find your door open, and caught someone ransacking your home. You confronted him, but he had a knife. It's all too common a tale, and no one will have any reason to doubt it…"

"But... But why are you doing this? What have I ever done to you?" Kees tried not to panic. The tone of Piet's voice had sent a chill through his blood, and he knew the man would have no qualms about stabbing him.

"Don't take this personally, *Meneer* van der Veer, but you'd never have found yourself in this position if you weren't fucking that freak."

"What are you talking about?"

"Arjan de Wit. You're fraternizing with the enemy. I mean... How you can stand to have that...that thing kiss you, paw you, share a bed with you, knowing what he really is?"

Piet jabbed the point of the knife at the side of Kees' neck, and Kees bit back a whimper. "Please, don't do this..."

"Or is that the turn-on?" Piet went on. "The fact he's not human. Tell me, does he change when you fuck? Could you really be the kind of sick pervert who enjoys having sex with a lion?"

"*What?*" Kees increased his struggles, desperate to get away from the man and his vile insinuations. He could never contemplate having the kind of relationship with Arjan that Piet suggested. "No, I don't... I couldn't. How can you believe that of me?"

"Well, y'know, I just wondered what the fascination could be. Wondered why you'd choose a shape-shifting weirdo like him when there are plenty of normal guys you could go for."

How does he know that Arjan's a shifter? As Kees asked himself the question, the answer became all too obvious.

"You... You're De Jager, aren't you?" Now he realized why the face of the man who'd attacked him outside Arjan's building had seemed so familiar. De

Roy had done his best to conceal his identity by wearing the scarf and the hood but Kees had seen into his eyes, even if he'd mistaken them for those of Eline Vos' boyfriend, Simon. "You killed Danny and the others, and you stabbed Lise."

"Congratulations. You may claim the grand prize." Piet's words dripped sarcasm. "And before you ask, I have no regrets—apart from not finishing the job with that Swedish shifter bitch. And I intend to succeed where those who came before me failed. I'm going to drive the pride out of Amsterdam, once and for all."

"That'll never happen. When Arjan finds out what's happened to me, he'll hunt you down."

"Oh, did I not tell you how the sad little story of your untimely death unfolds?"

Again, the tip of the knife pressed against his jugular, hard enough this time to break the skin. Kees felt blood trickle down to soak into the neckband of his T-shirt.

"Arjan de Wit will be so overcome with grief that he'll take a handful of pills and wash it down with a bottle of finest Dutch *jenever*. In his suicide note, he'll tell the world he's sorry, but he just can't live without you."

"You can't do this." Even to his own ears, Kees sounded like a man begging for his life. "You're meant to uphold the law."

"When it comes to keeping this beautiful city safe, ridding it of shifters *is* the law. At least as far as my family is concerned—and the other families who understand the true nature of the threat that walks among us in human form..."

The door to the apartment opened. Kees looked over to see Arjan enter the living room and start walking through to the kitchen, only to come to a halt as he took in the nature of the tableau before him.

"And here he is," Piet said. "The real star of the show. So glad you could join us, Arjan. You're just in time to watch me slit your lover's throat."

As he spoke, he raised the knife so that it now rested against Kees' Adam's apple.

Kees closed his eyes and offered up a silent prayer. When he opened them again, it was to see Arjan bounding forward. The transformation was so swift, Kees hardly believed it possible. One moment, a man came toward them. The next, he saw a full-grown lion, its fangs bared.

Arjan's breath was hot where it touched Kees' skin. Kees did his best to scramble free of Piet's grasp, not wanting to be caught in the middle of this fight. Piet dropped the knife, and reached for the gun he kept in the holster around his waist.

In the instant before Arjan snapped his jaws shut around his throat, the policeman loosed off a shot. It struck the lion in the right shoulder. Arjan's howl of rage and pain filled the apartment. It was the last thing Kees heard before he was pitched to the floor, striking his head hard, and blacked out.

* * * *

"So when exactly did you realize de Roy was De Jager?" Kees asked.

He lay in Arjan's bed, enjoying the quiet, reflective moments that followed a long, slow bout of lovemaking. Even though Arjan had claimed to feel no lingering after-effects from the shooting, Kees had made sure to find a position that put no weight on the shifter's injured arm.

"Only when I got that message from you. If I'd learned his full name before, I could have taken him out before he attacked Lise. Because it was always going to come down to that, you know. Him against me. But it seemed fate decreed I would only deal with Inspector Engelen."

"You have to give de Roy credit," Kees said grudgingly. "He was clever. I mean... Look at the way he timed his entrance at the crime scene the night Danny was killed so it looked like he'd been on another call, when I bet all the time he was busy abandoning the car and setting fire to it."

"Oh, yes, his job gave him the perfect opportunity to hide in plain sight. He had enough experience of forensics to make Anneke's death look like suicide and Wim's a case of natural causes, not murder. And I'm sure if any evidence appeared that might have incriminated him, he'd have made sure it went missing."

Kees thought of the fragment of knife blade that had been retrieved from Lise de Wit during her surgery. He could just picture Piet taking it from the doctor and telling him he'd get it to the forensic lab, while pocketing it to dispose of later. And always with that cocky little smile on his face. The man must have genuinely believed he would never get caught, and that if he did, the influence of the wealthy families who supported him would ensure he was not convicted.

"So what happens now?"

"Well, the police will investigate, of course, but after I told them we caught him going through your possessions and he turned the gun on us, I think they'll accept my plea that I only acted in self-defense. We grappled, the weapon went off, and the bullet grazed my shoulder before making a rather nasty mess of his throat." Arjan smiled, but there was no mirth in his expression. "Because if there's one thing they don't like, it's evidence that one of their own is corrupt—even if they don't know all the ways in which he was breaking the law."

Arjan wrapped his arm tighter around Kees.

"And the worst part is," Kees said, "he really seemed to believe he was doing the right thing."

He'd never told Arjan all the insults de Roy had spat out, all the nasty allusions he'd made to the nature of their relationship, and he suspected he never would.

"Let's not talk about him, Kees. Not when we need to talk about us."

Kees drew in a breath. He'd thought about deferring his return to the States by a couple of days, but Arjan's unnaturally speedy recovery had meant there'd been no need to change his immediate plans. But what happened between him and Arjan in the longer term still hung in the balance.

"What about us?" He tried to sound nonchalant.

"That first night in hospital, when you sat by my bedside... I'm sure you thought I'd fallen asleep, because you said a few things I don't think you ever intended me to hear."

"I'm sure I don't know what you mean." Kees hoped Arjan had not noticed the flush on his cheeks as he recalled how he'd spilled his feelings into the stillness of the hospital room.

"So you don't remember saying that you couldn't bear to live on the other side of the world without me? That you wished you could find some way of staying here?"

"Well... I might have."

"Don't be ashamed, Kees. I know how hard it can be to own up to your true feelings. But I've been speaking to Inspector Engelen, and it seems the force is looking to take on recruits to become part of their computer forensics team. And for a man with your level of expertise..."

"What? You're suggesting I join the police?"

"Think about it. You've shown you have an aptitude for detective work, you're a firm believer in justice and, most of all, you'd look really hot in uniform." He grinned. "And I'm sure my parents would be impressed by the fact my partner had such a respectable job."

"Your parents?"

"I want you to meet them before you leave for New York. I want you by my side when I tell my father I'm going to accept the role of pride leader. Things are about to get crazy in my life, and being with you will offer me the stability I'm going to need."

"But I can't pack up my life in New York just like that. There's my job to sort out. I'd have to sell my apartment..." He knew he sounded like he was making excuses.

"I'm sure you could leave that in the hands of a good real estate agent," Arjan said, "but all I really need to know right now is that you see a future with me."

"Oh, yes," Kees replied fervently. His doubts on that front had receded since the dreadful moments when Piet de Roy had tried to kill him. Arjan had been there when he'd needed him most and had risked his own life to save him. He knew he couldn't walk away from this man.

"Then let's make a sign of our commitment." Arjan fumbled in his bedside drawer and drew out something Kees recognized. Something that made him laugh out loud. A seashell pink and white plastic ring.

As he slipped it on to Kees' finger, Arjan said, "This is just a symbol. I'll find something better while you're in New York. How do you feel about a platinum band?"

A small, shameless part of Kees would have been happy to wear the cock ring, with all its thrilling reminders of their sleazy behavior in the toilets of Hemel en Aarde. But he said, "That sounds perfect." For the first time, he felt able to open up his heart and reveal the true depths of his feelings to Arjan. "*Ik hou van jou.*"

"I love you, too, Kees, and I always will."

As Arjan's lips met his in a long, tender kiss, Kees knew he was finally home. In the city of his heart, with the man he would always love. And at that moment, as the golden light of the Amsterdam evening streamed into the bedroom, there was nowhere he would rather be.

About the Author

Elizabeth Coldwell is the author of numerous short stories and two full-length novels, 'Calendar Girl' and 'Playing The Field'. Her stories have appeared in the best-selling 'Best Women's Erotica' series and Black Lace's popular 'Wicked Words' collections. Formerly the editor of the UK edition of Forum magazine, she now contributes a spicy monthly column, 'The Cougar Chronicles', to its pages. When she is not busy writing, she is an avid supporter of Rotherham United Football Club and can be regularly found on the terraces at weekends, cheering her boys to victory (hopefully!).

Elizabeth Coldwell loves to hear from readers. You can find her contact information, website details and author profile page at http://www.totallybound.com.

Totally Bound Publishing